# When Summer Turns to Fall

# Gary J. Gemme

## A Novel

1

# Copyright

LCCN: 2020901134

ISBN: 9781709967719

*To my children, grandchildren,*

*and to*

*Donna, the love of my life*

*as always*

*and*

*forever...*

# *Acknowledgements*

As an independent author my entourage of editors, researchers, cover designers, back page writers, marketeers, and tech savvy, social media professionals is small. My team is made up of a very supportive family. First and foremost, my wife Donna, with her Doctoral Degree, is a tough first reader. I would like to thank her for the time she spent reading and critiquing my manuscript. Michael, my editor, is an English teacher with a Master of Fine Art from the University of New Orleans. I thank him for helping his dad make, *When Summer Turns To Fall* a more enjoyable read. As always, he has my appreciation and gratitude. Thank you to my childhood friend, Mark Tonelli, for his help with the front and back cover photographs.

Given the shrinking platform of traditional publishing, with agents as gatekeepers, Amazon's Kindle Direct Publishing offers a rare opportunity for writers to realize their potential. I humbly thank all those involved in making KDP possible for independent writers to publish their work.

I don't have the words to fully express my appreciation to all the "Nightingales" who work on Eight West, the Bone Marrow Unit and Clinic at UMassMemorial Medical Center who made my stay, truly a home away from home. Thank you all for gracing me with your kindness and dedication.

Finally, thank you to rest of my loving family, Matthew, Jessica, Angelo, Gianna, Natalia, Luciana, Angelo Joseph, Meghan, Everly, and Juliet.

*The Road Not Taken*

By

Robert Frost


*Two roads diverged in a yellow wood*

*And sorry I could not travel both*

*And be one traveler, long I stood*

*And looked down one as far as I could*

*To where it bent in the under growth;*


*Then took the other, as just as fair*

*And having perhaps the better claim,*

*Because it was grassy and wanted wear;*

*Though as for that, the passing there*

*Had worn them really about the same.*


*And both that morning equally lay*

*In leaves no step had trodden black.*

*Oh! I kept the first for another day!*

*Yet knowing how way leads on to way,*

*I doubted if I should ever come back.*


*I should be telling this with a sigh*

*Somewhere ages and ages hence;*

*Two roads diverged in a wood and I –*

*I took the one less traveled by,*

*And that has made all the difference.*

# Table of Contents

# 1

Summer ended quickly, and, with it, the tidal wave of tourists. The seamless transition into the tranquil and peaceful autumn season, with its subtle changes in foliage, was the start of my first year as a wash-ashore. However one takes the meaning of the term wash-ashore, for the native, those not born and raised on Cape Cod—the definition is clear, you're an outsider.

I don't mind being considered an outsider; it's comfortable for me. I've never stayed in a place long enough to be an insider. Don't get me wrong, those born on the Cape are friendly enough, but you sense there's a wall around them, particularly with us wash-ashores, since we're competition for good jobs and affordable housing. To the natives, the tourist is a source of revenue, their survival; tolerable. Working class Cape Codders don't make ends meet with a single job, they tend to juggle two or three when the tourists are spending at leisure. After the summer season ends, it's an anxious survival to stay afloat.

My landing on Cape Cod was not planned, I simply ran out of road traveling from the west heading east, zig-zagging across the lower forty-eight states. It was a voyage that took me to the towns, cities, and sights of the places I'd read about during long stretches at sea.

Then unexpectedly, on a cold, stormy night I found comfort on Cape Cod. The wind, rain, thunder, and lighting pounding on the cottage I'd rented was like a call for all-hands-on-deck. Suddenly awakened, I quickly dressed, grabbed my foul-weather gear from my duffle bag, rushed to my pickup truck, and drove to West Dennis Beach. When I arrived, I made my way to the end of the wet, slick, rocky jetty. Standing strong, as if holding the night-watch; crashing waves washed over me and torrential rain beat on me like hailstones from a winter gale. Staring at the turbulent horizon, a serenity overtook me, I felt as if I was back at sea.

When I returned to my rented cottage, I slept the sleep of the dead. When finally awoke, I knew instinctively, the road I would take and the new home I had found. My resolve was now fixed, so I planned for a productive day. I was roaring to go by mid-morning, not unusual for a sailor assigned to a night watch. As a newly ordained civilian, since receiving my Honorable Discharge and Navy pension nearly nine months ago, I felt an urgency and didn't want time to wither away. This one weary traveler would not stand still, the road "less traveled" awaited me.

Some habits will never be broken; morning coffee strong, hot, and black. The caffeine jolt was followed by a daily jaunt. I'd rented a small shack off South Village Road, a short clip to Lower County Road. This was where I started my morning run. The sights quickly get scenic as you turn onto Lighthouse Road. Uncle Stephens Pond is on the right and Weirs Creek Pond the left. As I continued on my run, I entered into West Dennis Beach. A captivating, mile strip wedged between the cold blue-gray waters of Nantucket Sound and the salt marsh of Bass River.

The morning after the horrific storm, the sun had radiated the brilliance of a stage light illuminating a grand production; its beam highlighting the beauty of the baby-blue sky, the virgin-white clouds, the steely-colored water, and the faint foam surfing atop rolling waves. All too beautiful for words, but not for the Divine painter, who created a natural scene on the earth's canvas with skill and a palette with the most common colors.

After I completed the hard run, I ended with a walk to the tip of the jetty and stood where land ends and water begins; the same spot where I realized I'd found my new home. I had often made my way to the ship's deck the day after weathering a horrific storm. There's an unblemished beauty when surrounded by calm seas and an early morning sunrise. For this deckhand, the world always seemed free of the everyday noise and pressures of life. A momentary pleasure, I never wanted to lose.

I walked back to the cottage after leaving the jetty. While walking my observations were much clearer as my pace transcended to a shuffle. It was captivating taking in the wildflowers lining the sand flats and salt marshes bordering West Dennis Beach. Gazing out over the skyline I became enthralled watching the aeronautical prowess of various species of birds. Their theatrics in flight capture the uniqueness of nature. The Airforce's "Thunderbirds," while impressive, pale in comparison.

There were discreetly positioned, and oftentimes missed, well-presented ecological and environmental information posted along the ponds and marshes. A source of enlightenment that helped me to truly appreciate the habitat engulfing this oasis.

When I arrived at the cottage, I immediately drew up a checklist for my new plan. After nine months of travel, it was time to deliver this baby to his new home. First things first, a quick shower and shave, then off to see Kitten.

Kitten O'Leary, fifties, attractive, blond hair, plump with personality, and most of all, she knows the Cape. Kitten is a life-long long resident and the realtor who rented me my cottage. She's loveable from the first time you meet her. Sassy, quick witted, and you immediately know who's boss. Kitten, these days, is mostly into real estate sales, but she still cuts hair for her regulars; and when things get slow, she tells me, "Sailor Boy, I can still pass the suds with the prettiest of these young, beach girls."

Like I said, you can't help loving Kitten.

There was no need to call, I headed over to her office. Easy to find, it's the same as her home. She's always there and always on the phone. I walked in needing no introduction.

"Well there's my sexy Sailor, all shaven and everything, expecting me to head out on a date. You young men just want to take advantage of us pretty girls."

"Good afternoon Kitten, you know you're a local treasure, and a wash-ashore like me would rock these waters if I was so bold as to date the Cape's most treasured beauty."

"You're a charmer, Mikey, and full of wind. I'd look mighty royal, like Kate holding onto William's arm. Only with you, I'd be brushing up against your lean, six-foot frame, and a gorgeous couple we'd make. But, I've sworn off younger men, you all want a ring on my finger and the money in my bank account."

"Ah, Kitten my love, you've got me pegged right."

"So, what brings a handsome man with those sexy, soft, hazel eyes to see me on such a beautiful day." As Kitten spoke, she paused and looked at me intently. Her eyes penetrating, assessing, intuitive, not waiting for a response, she said, "Wait a minute, I can see it in your eyes, I can see it in your face. And now, a great big grin. You're spellbound! Spellbound with the Cape! Well, well, well, I'll be, I guess this is a business call, Michael Maine. So, let me put my realtor hat on and see how I can help you find your new home."

# 2

There was no buyer's remorse for this sailor and no other path for "another day." I'd washed ashore and Cape Cod was now my new home. Kitten went right to work finding me my first house. She promptly located the perfect run-down, fixer-upper in the Town of Dennis. On the plus side, I had a working bathroom, a place to sleep, and a heck of a lot of work to keep me busy. For the first time in twenty years I feel my roots are firmly planted in solid soil, and in a place where I know I belong.

Kitten gave me an overview of the historical area where my new house sits. When we sealed the deal on the property, Kitten, with her quick wit and historical knowledge of the Cape, said, "Sailor Boy, you're now the proud owner of property sitting on land originally part of the Hartley farm and a tale dating back to the 1860s." She went on to give me a history lesson of Old Man Hartley and the myth and mystery surrounding the farm.

The Hartley farm is tightly woven into the New England Gale of 1869, later named the Saxby Gale. The storm, with hurricane force winds, was the worst tropical cyclone to ever hit Cape Cod. On the eighth of September, a Wednesday afternoon, the vicious gale swept through the Mid-Cape causing devastation and destruction. By early evening, hurricane force winds were accompanied by a heavy-rainfall and widespread flooding.

The Hartley farm was overwhelmed by horrific winds and blinding sheets of rain. The storm washed away small sheds, barns, and completely destroyed the main house. When the floodwaters finally receded, Old Man Hartley and his wife Mary were missing and presumed dead. Remnants of the destroyed structures were scattered over the salt marsh bordering Sesuit Creek. Many believed the watery bog hosts the Hartley's unsettled bodies and souls.

Legend has it that Old Man Hartley was a loud, unfriendly, and an eccentric with a mean streak that made one's skin crawl as if insects were creeping over your body. He was not known as a friendly or welcoming neighbor, an anomaly in such a tight-knit community typical of the mid-eighteen hundreds.

After the estate was settled, the land was immediately broken up into various sized parcels with new houses sprouting up on both sides of Old King's Highway. Today, the scenic road is also known as Route 6A, Main Street, or simply 6A. My property faces the historical roadway and the rear of the house borders the salt marsh of Sesuit Creek. The sale of the Hartley property in the early 1870s allowed the growing community to expand. The increasing migration populated by small farmers, maritime industries, and merchants selling a variety of wares now had land for much needed housing.

As ghost stories are typically told, Old Man Hartley crawls out of the marsh and wanders the confines of his farm whenever the rains are torrential, and the winds howl with the acoustics of a coyote in the wilderness. The story has grown over the years with talk of strange happenings and frightening occurrences. The many acres once part of Hartley's property are now considered haunted. My lot is situated in the middle of the old farm, nestled against the fabled mire.

I'm not one for ghost stories, but I appreciated the historical and legendary tale Kitten had exhaustively provided. I had too much work ahead of me to dwell on Old Man Hartley or the myth and mystery surrounding the disappearance and death of the Hartleys. My priority was to get started on making my fixer-upper a livable home.

My renovations started with a visit to the Center-Cape Home Store to purchase the tools and materials needed to begin my remodeling project. I was introduced to Tom, a knowledgeable building specialist. He was generous with his time, tremendously helpful, and guided me throughout my project. Experience had taught me the right tool makes the task easier and the work more gratifying. Starting the project with Tom's help made for smooth sailing.

Tom is one of those Cape Cod characters with his own signature sense of humor. He loves to dish out remodeling advice with a contradictory twist of his words. His two favorite guiding quotes, he never fails to say are, "Remember Mike, Righty-loosey-lefty-tighty... hah, hah, hah." He offers me this sage advice every time we're in the plumbing department. When I'm buying wood products his favorite is, "Mike, I know I don't need to remind you, but remember, measure once, cut twice… hah, hah, hah." Tom's a good guy with a unique personality and despite his comedic deficiency, a heck of a knowledgeable guy.

The first order of business was to repair the outdoor shower. After spending twenty years in the Navy, I've taken my share of open-air showers and I willingly embraced the Cape Cod tradition of bathing under the heavenly sky. For those of you who've never experienced the exhilaration of water jetting from a showerhead while standing in the fresh air and sunshine, you're missing an opportunity to experience one of those small treats that gives life buoyancy; an exuberance, like listening to the crashing surf while your body cuts through the whitecaps with the sun's brilliance shining on your back. The most enjoyable experience is showering outside on a cold, misty, rainy day. The hot spray from the nozzle, mixed with the mist and frosty air, is like diving into a frigid breaker when the sun is hibernating.

With the outdoor shower and enclosure completed, it was time to tackle serious remodeling. My days started with a strong coffee, a quick run, and as you may suspect, an open-air shower. I try not to waste water, but there are no more Navy-imposed two minute showers for this retired sailor.

On most days, I would head over to the Yellow Cottage, on Old Bass River Road, for breakfast. I made a point of arriving at seven in the morning when the restaurant first opened. I could usually grab a seat at the counter with the locals. After a few weeks, my presence was a familiar sight and the ice was broken. I started to become acquainted with the regulars who dominated the counter conversation. Making friends with Ed, the cook, a quick-witted, talkative guy and with most of the waitresses was pretty easy.

I'm friendly and engaging myself, so it was nice to begin to develop a relationship with some of the residents of Dennis and the surrounding area. Most of the early morning patrons were contractors, small business owners, or workers who started their day with breakfast and a little camaraderie at the Yellow Cottage.

I tried to spend my money at locally owned businesses to support their livelihood. It was also a way to develop relationships that made me feel like part of the community. My truck needed gas, so I frequented a place at the corner of Main and Bank Street in Harwich. It's a little out of the way, but Marco owns the Speed-A-Way Service Station and is a Navy Veteran. He's five years older, my height, and carries thirty pounds more muscle than me. He keeps his hair cut short, is good looking with light olive skin inherited from his Spanish and Italian grandparents. Marco flies the US and Navy flags at his station. We connected instantly and developed a friendly relationship. Since we shared similar experiences, the bantering came quick and easy.

It was nice to meet people where you develop a rapport, joke, and jest. My approach when dealing with most people is to speak less and listen more. Through experience, I've learned that taking an honest interest in other people's words helps build friendships. The locals, when you get to know them, are usually witty and welcoming. Once accepted, you start to meet some of the colorful characters who make up the Cape, and slowly you begin to become a part of the community.

My love of reading brought me to the Dennis Public Library, where I met Rachael Morgan. I read a short "Know-Your-Librarian" bio on her and learned she spent twelve years with the FBI as an analyst and turned librarian when she moved to Cape Cod. To be honest, I fell head-over-heels when I first introduced myself to her.

Rachael, I guessed was slightly younger than me, in the range of thirty-six to thirty-seven. She looked to be about five feet six inches, black hair cut short, slim, and has stunning brown eyes. She's smart, friendly, and funny; and a beauty, way-way out of my league. I'm like a boomerang, returning to the library regularly. The services are outstanding, but most of all, I go and act like a sophomore sneaking peeks at the high school beauty.

Rachael is well-read and a tremendous source of knowledge. She reintroduced me to the classics and required reading from my high school days. Some of her favorite books included *To Kill a Mockingbird, The Catcher and the Rye, Wuthering Heights,* and *For Whom the Bell Tolls.* Some of the authors she recommended were William Faulkner, Edward Jones, Corman McCarthy, and Maxine Hong Kingston. Many of these novels brought me back to a different time and place. Reading them as an adult, and as a critical reader, gave me a better understanding of the books I'd read so long ago and didn't appreciate.

With the progress I'd made on the rehab project, I started to venture out in the evenings. My time was balanced between relaxing at the library and grabbing a bite to eat at the local pubs. I much preferred the library where I could read, talk with Rachael, and steal unsuspected gazes at her. I'd made subtle inquiries with her co-workers and learned Rachael was single and not dating anyone special. Every visit to the library, I became more smitten with her, but I didn't have the courage to ask her out. I also didn't want to inhibit our friendly relationship with an obvious overreach on my part.

My evenings dining out weren't what you'd describe as "fine dining." I'd settled on Bunny's Sports Café and the Mad Dawg Pub. Two moderately priced restaurants with a diverse menu to satisfy this hungry sailor. My approach with the people hanging out at these taverns, was the same as I'd used at the Yellow Cottage. After weeks of sitting quietly at the bar, eating a meal, and having a Bud or two (this guy's limit), I was accepted as a regular. It's funny how these relationships start, it begins with a nod, turns into a "Hey" or "How ya doin," to small talk, and then, light bantering. It wasn't long before I was getting a full dose of witticisms from the regular characters. The bartenders and waitresses were like emissaries of goodwill. You could always count on them to be friendly, hospitable, and informative about local events, sprinkled with tidbits of gossip. The atmosphere reminded me of the old sitcom *Cheers*, "Where everybody knows your name."

I'm sure you're wondering about my romantic pursuits. I'd had plenty of opportunities to date, but like I said, I'm head over heels for Rachael. If there was one thing this guy learned in the Navy, it was patience. With my favorite librarian, I subscribed to the old adage, "Anything (or anyone) worth having, is worth waiting for."

Back at the homestead, I continued to work hard repairing my house. To tell you the truth, I didn't need to buy a fixer-upper. For me though, the rehab project kept me busy while I honed my remodeling skills. Plus, I was proud of using my hands to turn a rundown shack into a cozy home.

As the weeks passed, my social life (if you want to call it that) was flatlined, but that was good with me. I still had hoped the sun would shine every day and Rachael would lower her standards and see something worthy in this retired sailor.

There were two other priorities I still needed to address. One was my palate and the other, my hair. The first order of business was to buy myself a grill. While the food at the pubs was good, I wanted the enjoyment of firing up the grill cooking fish, chicken, or an occasional steak. So, I headed over to the local hardware store on Route 134 in Dennis and bought myself a three burner Weber. The staff was helpful, informative, and the price reasonable. I loaded the grill into the bed of the truck and couldn't wait to enjoy my first home cooked meal over hot flames.

As a career navy man my hair was always cut short and hardly current. With Rachael in mind, I wanted to find a place that would give me a contemporary look, and an age appropriate haircut. After asking the locals I'd befriended, I settled on the New-Do Hair Salon on Old Bass River Road in Dennis. There I met Sarah, who took me under her wing. She's a native, smart, and funny. Sarah knew what I was looking for, and in no time had my thirty-eight--year-old hair cut fashionably.

"What do you think of your new look, Michael. It's sort of a retro style and fits your face well. I kept it short around the ears, faded the sides for a nice blend, and left the top long enough for you to comb it to the side. We can play around with the length until you're comfortable with the look. I added a touch of gel to give you a shiny, healthy look."

"Wow, it looks great Sarah, I appreciate it."

"Well, if you want to maintain a stylish, handsome look, you're going to need to come in regularly."

"I'll come in every week if I can maintain this style. After twenty years of Navy regulation haircuts, I feel like a new man."

"I'm sure the women in your life will appreciate your new image."

"There's no woman in my life but…"

"We can fix that without any difficulty, somebody as sexy as you."

"Thanks Sarah, I'll keep your confidence in mind."

"Don't be so shy, Michael."

"It's been awhile since I dated someone regularly."

"You must have your eye on a hot babe."

"It's a 'Hail Mary' pass, and the odds are against me."

"Next time you're in, I'll be checking the score."

After paying Sarah and scheduling my next appointment, I headed out to enjoy the day. Things were going well, and I relished my new life in a place where I was definitely fitting in. That evening, I used my new grill for the first time. A piece of salmon was on the menu, and I savored the taste of the Pacific fish.

After cleaning up, I spent time at the library gawking at Rachael, while distractedly reading. No way I could concentrate, particularly after Rachael gave me a double take when she saw me and said, "Very nice haircut, Michael, quite the contemporary look."

My cool response was to stand tongue tied and blushing like a teenager. Further transporting me to the ice age was her smile as she walked away. I almost had to give myself chest compressions to get my blood moving. I don't know how I'm going to develop a rapport with Rachael when her smile turns me as motionless as Michelangelo's sculpture *David*.

Despite my lack of savoir faire in the presence of my favorite librarian, I went to bed on the twenty-fifth of November with a feeling of serenity. When my head hit the pillow, a deep sleep overcame me. Before the clock struck midnight everything would change as high winds and sheets of blinding rain inundated the Mid-Cape area. When a thunderous boom shook the house, suddenly, I was wide awake.

I quickly donned my foul weather gear and headed outdoors. The winds were raging and the rain relentless. Visibility was blurred as if trying to see through opaque glass. Without hesitation, I secured the new gas grill and locked the patio furniture into the outdoor shower stall for protection. I've been out at sea during storms like this and took all the precautions of a sailor on a ship. With everything fastened, I returned to the house. The windows were rattling from fierce winds and the power was out. I have a generator but decided to wait until morning or for the rains to stop before starting it up.

When I had gone back into the house I was still wearing my rain gear. As fatigue crept up on me, the couch turned into a welcoming bed. When I awoke around dawn, the rains had stopped. There was an unusual, eerie, stillness in the air. I lay motionless trying to gain some perspective on last night's events before assessing the damage.

After climbing off the couch I checked the interior of the house, and except for the power outage everything looked intact. Once outdoors I walked around the perimeter of the property and noticed there were plenty of roof shingles that would need to be replaced. I'd lost two trees, but my shed was undamaged, and the house needed only minor repairs. I went back inside to check the power, but it was still out, so I started the portable generator. At least I had limited lighting, the refrigerator working, and heat for the house.

I went back outdoors to recheck the property and noticed a rusty piece of metal in the wet grass just beyond the patio. When I bent down to pick it up it wouldn't budge. I used my hands to dig around the object and loosen the soil's hold on it. Once out of the cold, muddy ground, I recognized it as an old Mason jar with a metal lid. I wiped away the dirt from the glass to get a better look inside, and there appeared to be a folded piece of paper in the container. I brought the jar into the house and tried to remove the metal top. The lid was frozen tight and wouldn't budge. I went out to the shed, grabbed my toolbox, and a can of WD-40 in an attempt to salvage the jar without breaking the glass.

When I returned to the house, I sprayed oil around the circumference of the metal cover. After several minutes the oil worked its way between the glass and the metal. With the aid of a plumber's wrench and an abundance of patience, the metal lid slowly turned open. I carefully lifted the paper from the jar and unfolded it. To my astonishment, it was a letter signed by Mary Hartley. After recovering from my initial shock, I read the neat, tidy handwriting.

*September 8, 1869*

*The rains started & the wind is blowing hard. The Old Man is acting strange he is quoting scriptures about the end of the world. I am afraid, he is outside digging around the shed between the barn & the house. He has been ranting & raving about a burial plot. I am so scared I am not sure what he will do. He came into the house wet to his bones quoting Matthew about angels & heaven & not knowing when. Now Luke about the sun & the moon & roaring seas with waves people fainting with foreboding of what is coming. He is now back outside the winds & rain keep coming & we lost some trees & now the roof is off the shed. The Old Man is screaming & chanting I can't hear what he is saying I barely see him with the rain pouring down. He is back in the house I hardly recognize him. Now he is yelling telling me the Lord is coming like a thief in the night. The house is shaking the roof has torn away & water is flowing into the house. We lost the shed it washed away. The Old Man keeps shoveling I am so afraid. If I should die tonight I beg for a Christian burial for I am a Catholic my soul needs a home. The barn is gone we lost the windows the house is breaking apart. The Old Man is back I don't recognize him for he is in a foolish rage. He is screaming Matthew 24, & Armageddon he said the end of the world is at hand. The Old Man just ran out of the house he is digging with a fury. I am putting this letter in a mason jar I beg for a Christian burial & absolution for my sins if I should die this night. Please Lord forgive my transgressions.*

 *Mary Hartley*


 After regaining my composure, I reread the letter until I nearly memorized it. I silently asked myself: "Was the letter really written by Mary Hartley? Was it possible for the letter to remain intact after 150 years? Was there a way to honor her wish? Could her remains be found?" All these questions, without answers, ran through my mind.

Initially I wasn't quite sure how to proceed. Thinking about it, I knew I needed to show the letter to Rachael and Kitten, but with the holiday season approaching, I felt it best to wait until after Christmas. If I was going to make a commitment to honoring Mary's request, I still needed to repair the damage caused by the storm and finish remodeling. This would require most of my time during the remainder of the month. The letter had stayed in the forefront of my mind, while I tried to concentrate on the work I needed to complete. With three-and-one-half weeks until the twenty-fifth, I had my work cut out for me.

\*

My piece of Cape Cod sits on a twenty-five thousand square foot lot. The parcel is narrow, runs deep, and abuts the salt marshes of Quivett Creek. From my vantage point, the backyard and beyond is a natural wildlife sanctuary.

The house is one-thousand and eighty square feet. I love the coziness of my new home. I have two bedrooms and one-and-a-half bathrooms. There's a good size kitchen and a large front room. I turned the sunroom into an all-purpose room with a couch, television, and a table where I can sit and eat my meals.

I set up four bird feeders and two bird baths near the remnants of an old stone wall in the rear of my property. My all-purpose room provided a terrific view of the wide variety of birds frequenting the backyard. Immediately, as if by a magnet's pull, there was plenty of activity at the feeders with the daily appearance of cardinals, blue jays, and other local birds. I also have a family of wild turkeys and a bunch of menacing squirrels aggressively attacking the feeders. This gang of critters consumes a forty-pound bag of seeds a week, and premium blend to boot. Overall, I have a wonderful vantage point, with plenty of space for a single guy who doesn't expect many guests.

With the remodeling work I needed to complete; it gave me an opportunity to distance myself from my regular routine. I spent less time at the Mad Dawg Pub and at Bunny's Sports Café, and more time fixing up my house. With a lot of effort, and laboring long days, the repairs and makeover were finished by Christmas. When one on the local businesses had a holiday special, I indulged and bought a central air conditioning system and a gas fireplace. There's no doubt, this Navy man could have been a woodchopper, but I love the convenience of the gas fireplace. A little AC during the heat of the summer won't be too bad either.

I made subtle inquiries at the library and learned Rachael was visiting relatives for the holidays. Rachael had once told me how much she loved the book *Dangerous Ambition* by Susan Hertog. I managed to track down a signed copy on the Internet. The book traces the lives of two women, Dorothy Thompson and Rebecca West, as they search for love and power. For obvious reasons, it was placed at the top of my list of books to read. I also came across a signed copy of Dorothy Thompson's 1938 Political Guide: *A Study of American liberalism and its Relationship to Modern Totalitarianism.* I couldn't resist buying both books for Rachael, and in my view, a two-hundred-dollar gift for a friend wasn't a big deal.

I dropped the presents off at the library when I knew Rachael wasn't working. I didn't want her to think she needed to reciprocate and buy me a gift. My plan was to stay away from the library until after Rachael left for her vacation. This sailor wasn't sure his emotions could handle a goodbye. My glassy eyes would have told Rachael I wanted more than a casual friendship with her, and I didn't think she was ready for that kind of commitment.

Seeing Kitten was a different story, she's always home, and readily accessible. I dropped off a pine wreath and a case of her favorite Bordeaux. She invited me to her house for Christmas dinner, but I told her I had company coming. She eyed me suspiciously but let the subject drop.

In fact, my company was a four-legged puppy, and not a person. I'd decided it was time for companionship; a dog makes the perfect "best friend." Buying the right breed was a tough decision. I had made a list of pups that would make a good companion and settled on a Labrador retriever. My challenge was trying to choose between a black, chocolate, or yellow one. Ultimately, the decision was not made by me. The deal was sealed when a golden-haired Lab nestled up to my leg and looked at me with his big round eyes. I paid the local dog breeder, and after the pup received all his shots, I brought my new roommate home.

According to the American Kennel Club, Labrador retrievers are friendly and outgoing, and play well with other dogs. They're also very active; Labs are high-spirited and not afraid to show it. That's good with me, it sort of fits my personality. They're trainable and under proper supervision, good with children. I named my pup Sailor, and there is no doubt, this former Chief Warrant Officer would be the skipper and Sailor the mate.

I spent a quiet twenty-fourth and fifth reading *The Greatest Christmas Stories of all Time,* to my little buddy, taking long walks, and mostly lounging in front of the gas fireplace. Like I said, a little convenience was what I was looking for, and, after spending the majority of my Navy career at sea, a little convenience was well earned.

Once I had Sailor home I began the slow process of house-training him. We took frequent walks, so I could teach him where to do his business. I also enjoyed playing with and training him to understand who's the deck hand and who's the skipper. Sailor was responsive and a quick learner. We were fast becoming shipmates, and I greatly enjoyed the company.

With the Christmas holiday over, and the new year a week away, it was time to return to Mary Hartley's letter. After rereading her plea, it got me pondering about the Ghost of Old Man Hartley and the unusual stillness I'd felt the day after the storm. Maybe there was something to the ghostly yarn after all, and it wasn't the specter of the Old Man wandering around the farm, but rather, Mary Hartley's spirit.

Before I approached Rachael and Kitten with the letter, I wanted to do enough research to give them a perspective of the challenges I would face trying to honor Mary's request. My navy training had taught me when you approach an unusual situation make a list of what you need to do to solve the problem. With Mary's letter, I needed more information; specifically, the layout of the farm, the Saxby Gale, and Catholicism of her era. Learning the history of Dennis could provide important leads about the Hartley property. An understanding of the farming community during the 1860s was a potential link to solving the mystery. The quality of the paper the letter was written on, and somehow preserved, piqued my interest about the canning process of the eighteen hundreds. There was a lot more I needed to know. I had at least a week to do my research before I showed Rachael and Kitten the letter.

Starting on the twenty-sixth, with Rachael still away, I spent a considerable amount of time at the library. During the evening, I returned to my usual haunts. Most nights, I was eating and hanging out at the Mad Dawg Pub or Bunny's. Unlike Christmas, when many of the bar regulars were solemn and showed little excitement for the holiday, or like me, had excuses for not being around; there was an exuberance about New Year's Eve. The unabashed zest for a wild celebration started the evening of December twenty-sixth.

I decided to spend New Year's Eve splitting my time between Bunny's and the Mad Dawg Pub. By eleven o'clock,

I wanted to be home with Sailor and welcome in the new year with my new first mate. I had zero enthusiasm for ringing in 2018, my first New Year's on the Cape, with a bunch of drunken acquaintances.

On the morning of the twenty-seventh of December, the list of topics I needed to research was completed. My first thought was to focus on the low hanging fruit and work my way up to the more time-consuming questions. The canning process had stimulated my interest, so I started there. Over the next week, I would also focus on the history of Dennis, the Saxby Gale, Catholicism on the Cape, and lastly, the Hartley Farm, The Old Man, and Mary.

The library and the Internet provided an abundance of information, especially Wikipedia. As a history buff, I appreciated the details of the canning process and the story of its development. According to Internet in general, and Wikipedia specifically, the canning process was developed by Nicolas Appert. He was a Frenchman who invented food preservation. In 1806, Appert presented Napoleon with a selection of airtight bottled fruits and vegetables. Appert's discovery provided Napoleon's troops with bottled food; a military advantage, placing his adversaries at a distinct disadvantage.

The canning process advanced significantly with the development of the Mason jar. According to Wikipedia, "In 1858, John Landis Mason invented a saguaro-shouldered jar with a threaded screw-top, metal lid, and rubber ring for an airtight seal—the Mason jar." In 1858, Mason patented the first screw top lid.

In 1861, the Mason jar was used by both the North and the South during the Civil War. It evolved into a reliable container for preserving nutritious food. The fruits and vegetables, protected in the sealed jars, became a source of nutrition augmenting the food supply for the troops; particularly during the winter months. By 1869, the Mason jar was widely used by the public at large.

This information convinced me Mary's letter was real and helped me to better understand why it was preserved and legible. When you read her text, you get a sense she was smart and articulate. She had the foresight to place her letter in a Mason jar in order to protect the message she'd written under extreme conditions. Mary expressed a strong commitment to her Catholic faith and deserves a Christian funeral service. The more I read her letter, the clearer my understanding of who Mary was as a person. This discernment made me determined to do all I could so that

Mary Hartley would be buried in the tradition of her faith—her soul should have a home.

When I hit my bunk, my thoughts were consumed with all the material I read. So, I laid awake and slowed my breathing to let my mind settle down before I nodded off to sleep. I perfected this method of clearing all the noise running through my head while in the Navy. Over the last twenty years, using this technique, I was able to get a good night's rest under the worst of circumstances.

I awoke the next morning with a vague notion of a voice faintly whispering, "Michael, it's Mary, you found my letter." Feeling well rested and highly motivated, I let the words slip into my subconscious without giving it much thought. Getting back to my research was my priority. After walking the little critter, I headed out for a swift run. I skipped my usual routine of walking home; instead made a loop and briskly returned to my house. I'd closed the outdoor shower in early November, so it was a hot indoor shower for this sailor. Refreshed, I dressed, grabbed a large black coffee from double Ds, and headed over to the library. I wanted to continue to dig into the history of Dennis. My hope was to learn how the town managed the land owned by the farming community. The goal was to identify the boundaries of the Hartley property, the layout of the physical structures that made up the farm, and possibly locate archives of neighboring families whose descendants may still be alive.

I began looking at historical periodicals and textbooks related to the early political periods. The first was the Plantation Period, which ran from 1830 to 1892. An Internet search and Wikipedia also provided me with an abundance of information to sort through. After separating the relevant from the nice to know, I'd learned the Barnstable Settlement was established in 1638. Dennis, at the time, was part of Yarmouth and settled in 1639; however, it remained unincorporated with boundaries finally set in 1692.

The Town of Dennis ultimately split from Yarmouth and was incorporated in 1793. Also, during the 1830s the population of Dennis began to grow with agriculture and farming the primary occupations. The population of Dennis in 1830 was 2,317, and by 1850, increased to 3,662 residents and was considered a large town.

This population growth reduced the amount of land for farming, so seafaring became the town's major industry. Navigation employment and maritime pursuits accounted for roughly seventy-four percent of the jobs. While agricultural employment decreased to around twenty percent. With a shrinking farming population, there may be helpful information about the Hartley's and their farm. This historical perspective made me optimistic that I would discover some clue to help me find the location of the shed where Old Man Hartley was shoveling.

Digging through a stack of old records and newspaper clippings, I came across a 1949 obituary of Rose (Roisin) Flynn, born 1847 in Ireland. The article highlighted the Flynn family's deep roots in the Town of Dennis. There was a quote from her 15-year-old great-granddaughter who mentioned, the deceased, one-hundred-two-year-old Rose had survived the Saxby Gale as a young woman. The obituary further stated the Flynn home, rebuilt after the great storm, still stands as a reminder of a bygone era and is on the National Register of Historic Places in Barnstable County.

I knew it was a long shot, but thought it was worth stopping by the address to see if the house was still there, and if the now eighty-five-year-old great-granddaughter resided at the historic family home. The Flynn house was a Greek Revival, originally built in the 1830s and a mile from my cottage. It's one of the imposing mansions lining sections of the Old King's Highway. You couldn't help admiring the grandeur of the Victorian Period. As I approached the front door; the dignity of the old structure with its dark, slate colored roof, pale yellow exterior, and black shutters was impressive. There was an aura of royalty; revered, honored, with a stateliness warranting the presence of a Swiss Guard. The bright sunlight radiated off the statuesque abode giving me a warm sensation. Suddenly, I was overcome by a strong feeling that I wasn't alone. My imagination overpowered reality when a hologram-like image of two young women appeared before me. The attractive couple were swaying on a porch swing, nestled together as if sharing secrets. The vision lasted only seconds but seemed real. I immediately attributed the warm joyfulness that came over me to my romantic notions of the magnificent house and Mary Hartley.

As luck would have it, a sprightly woman who looked to be in her 80s answered the door. After identifying myself and stating the purpose of my visit, Mrs. Irene Murphy confirmed she was the great-granddaughter of Rose Flynn. Mrs. Murphy invited me into her home that could best be described as a museum. The house was immaculate and the furniture dated from the late 1800s to the early 1900s. Mrs. Murphy pointed out an original painting of Rose and her husband that was prominently mounted over the fireplace. The portrait graced the expansive sitting room with an eminence that said, "We are more than just oil and canvas." Looking at the portrait, I immediately noticed Rose's wide, sparkling blue eyes. They seemed to lock on me like a laser beam. Under her imposing glare I didn't feel hostility; it was

45

more Rose could see right through me, as if assessing what was in my heart.

There was a large bouquet of red, white, pink, and yellow roses on the mantel and I said, "What exquisite roses, Mrs. Murphy."

"It's funny, rarely do I get a strong presence of my great-grandmother, but this morning I did. You know, for some reason, I went out and bought her four favorite color roses."

"They accentuate your great-grandmother's beauty."

"Thank you, I think so too."

"The artist created such beautiful eyes. They seem to look right through you."

"Oh, that wasn't a creation, the artist captured her eyes as they really were. She had such imposing eyes, you felt she knew what you were thinking. When she asked you a question, it was as if she already knew the answer. Needless to say, you didn't fib or lie to my great-grandmother."

"The artist's name is unreadable. I only see a faint outline of where there must have been a signature. Do you recall the name of the painter?

"I'm sorry, I don't."

Mrs. Murphy motioned for me to sit on one of a matching set of walnut, French Cane Back Chairs near a stained glass window. As we talked, she was quite enthusiastic once I explained the full purpose of my visit. She referred to the work I was doing as, "Your project." Mrs. Murphy spoke with joy, referring to her great-grandmother as a spiritual woman, somewhat mystical. She also told me she grew up hearing dreadful tales of the Saxby Gale. As a young girl, she would listen to stories of strange occurrences in the area of the destroyed, Hartley farm. Mrs. Murphy confessed to me that she never sleeps well on nights when the weather turns stormy and hard rain, coupled with roaring thunder rattles her old house.

Other than Catholics being a small community, she had only a vague recollection of hearing talk of Catholicism in the 1860s. She couldn't offer me much in terms of substance to help me in my quest for information needed to facilitate my investigation.

Mrs. Murphy did have a clear remembrance of Rose and Mary becoming good friends through their charitable work and Christian faith. She said, "I was constantly reminded by my great-grandmother that Mary Hartley was a good friend and a wonderful, caring person. She was extremely disturbed when her body was never recovered. Even as she lay dying, she told me, she didn't think she could rest in peace until Mary's soul was given a proper burial."

"Did your great-grandmother ever describe Mary or tell you anything more about her?"

"Oh yes, she described her as an extremely beautiful woman. Mary was twenty-five years younger than Old Man Hartley. From stories I'd heard, he was a wretched man. According to my great-grandmother their age difference wasn't unusual. Life expectancy, harsh conditions, and arranged relationships resulted in marriages of necessity."

"Mary must have had a difficult life."

"Most women during that period had hard lives. Farming was a family responsibility and difficult work."

"Can you remember anything else?"

"I remember towards the end of her life, when she was heavily medicated, she would talk of Mary. Most often, she didn't speak in complete sentences, only phrases. I recall her saying Mary had found happiness and that she had a secret. She never elaborated and of course, being a young girl, I was dying to know her secret."

After pausing, Mrs. Murphy continued and said, "As an art lover, my great-grandmother always lamented over the tragic loss of the original painting of the Hartley farm. The artist's impression captured the precise rendition of the landscape. The painter is the same artist who had painted the portrait of my great-grandparents that hangs over the fireplace. The young artist was on his way to a promising career until he went missing on that horrible night."

"Do you know who commissioned the Hartley Painting?"

"I remember my great-grandmother once saying Mary arranged it. When I questioned her further, she changed the subject."

"This may seem like an odd question, but did your great-grandmother and Mary ever spend time together on the front porch swing?"

"It's funny you should ask about the swing. My great-grandmother would occasionally stare at the swing, and when she did, a melancholy would overcome her. She would become very sad, saying how much she missed her dear friend Mary."

I didn't mention the illusion I had of the two women on the front porch swing. There was no point in exposing my wild, romantic, imagination to this wonderful woman.

\*

My talk with Mrs. Murphy left me with so many questions about Mary Hartley. I wanted to know as much as I could of her life and mostly her secret. While I hardly knew

Mary Hartley, speaking with Mrs. Murphy gave me a physical description and a perspective on her life. The information confirmed that my commitment to finding whatever remained of Mary's body was the right thing to do. I would continue my research with zeal and pursue every clue with equal energy.

My next step was to learn as much as I could about the Saxby Gale. I decided it was a task for the next day. I needed to get home to Sailor and take care of my list of neglected chores. That evening, I hit the usual haunts; my first stop was Bunny's for a quick Bud and then, a meal at the Mad Dawg Pub. I was home by nine with the fireplace aglow and my little buddy snuggling next to me. I had my head in a bundle of books I'd borrowed from the library. I was fixated on the great storm of 1869, reading until midnight. My enthusiasm had me wired, and I couldn't wait to return to the library in the morning and learn more.

You know how I start my day by now. Sailor gets to stretch his legs outdoors, I brew coffee hot, strong, and black, and in all types of weather I head out for a run. This was a morning when I could hear the starters gun go off. I sprinted out on a four-mile loop; picked up the pace at the back stretch, didn't let up on the far turn, and left nothing on the track down the homestretch. Hey, I didn't break any speed records, but this guy worked up a good sweat and within thirty minutes I was walking into my house.

I returned to the library when the doors opened. I had the usual large, black double D and my rucksack filled with books and notes. I immediately became engrossed in my research and learned; The Saxby Gale of 1869 was the last gale to hit New England. The day of the storm started out sunny and bright. At three-thirty that afternoon hurricane winds began to emerge and by five-thirty, the gale had increased. The hurricane raged that evening between eight and nine o'clock, with heavy sheets of rain coming down causing widespread flooding. The storm produced tremendous destruction, but ironically, generated the much-needed water to relieve a long, damaging drought.

The storm was considered a narrow one of less than fifty miles, but its violence ravaged Narragansett Bay, Buzzards Bay, and the Mid-Cape, including Dennis. The hurricane caused widespread havoc to houses, land, water, telegraph lines, trees, fences, chimneys, and caused numerous deaths. I came across a short poem written by John Wood titled, *The Saxby Gale.*

*Summers and summers have come, and gone with the flight of the swallow;*

*Sunshine and thunder have been, storm, and winter, and frost; Many and many a sorrow has all but died from remembrance,*

*Many a dream of joy fall'n in the shadow of pain.*

The heartfelt lines brought this retired Chief Warrant Officer to tears. I didn't need any more inspiration to solve this puzzle. There was no way I would forget Mary Hartley or the Saxby Gale.

It was four o'clock, and time to take Sailor for his afternoon walk. I was wound up by the whole Saxby Gale affair, so I made it a long one to tire out the pup and help me decompress. I wanted to get an early dinner at Bunny's, have a Bud, and get home to the little tyke and review all my notes. I was damn sure I would never forget Mary Hartley, a smart, courageous woman! I now had a dual incentive, Mary's soul needed a proper burial, so that her good friend Rose could finally rest in peace.

It's amazing what a good night's sleep will do to revive your body and mind. I woke up, had a coffee, took my mate outside for a stroll, and went for a long slow run, ending with a nice walk home. As I returned to my house, I hadn't paid attention to the beautiful nature surrounding me. My thoughts were fixated compulsively on Mary. Her voice was playing softly in my head, speaking with a whisper calling out to me, "Michael, Michael, It's Mary, can you hear me? Please help me." It was as if she had visited me in my sleep last night and I could feel the warmth of her physical presence. This may sound foolish, but in a way I was beginning to fall in love with her. She had so much inner strength, I wanted to believe her spirit was driving me.

I sat at the dining table letting my mind slowly review the information I'd collected. I knew the material was more inspirational than a key to solving the mystery of where Mary's skeleton could lay, but still, it gave me hope. I wanted to take it easy before heading to the library, so I played ball outdoors with Sailor until he was worn out. An unusual amount of activity at the bird feeders, for a cold December morning, caught my eye. I quickly grabbed my birder bag containing a notebook, several books for identifying birds, and binoculars. When I retired from the Navy I'd purchased the perfect field glasses for an aspiring birdwatcher. The Celestron, Trail Seeker binoculars came in handy during my nine-month tour, zigzagging across the country. A piece of equipment that I would put to good use on this wintery day.

I love birds, wildlife, nature preserves, parks, beaches, and flowers. I'm a tough guy and tough guys aren't sensitive, we never cry. Hah, hah, hah; once this Cat's emotions erupt, tears flow like lava from a volcano. I'd always kept my feelings in check during my Navy career, but since my discharge, I've become much more sentimental when it comes to nature.

Anyway, I'm a novice birder and will never get promoted to an amateur. I keep trying to recognize the same birds over and over again and can never remember which is which. It's like with flowers, I'll never, ever learn their names, but for me, it's the vividness of the colors—reds, blues, yellows, and purples that I'm fascinated by.

My knowledge of birds comes from the book, *Birds of Massachusetts, Field Guide,* by Stan Tekiela. It's a great guidebook; color coded, designed for the novice, and made easy, so you can quickly find the bird you're looking for. I renamed it, *The Bird Book for Dummies Like Me.*

The morning vanished in a flash, I spent ninety minutes as a birder; hah, an unlikely bird watcher status I'll never reach. This beginner quickly spotted a small, familiar bird with an orangey-red face and chest. You think I could remember the name. I had to grab my copy of Tekiela's book, and boom, I had the bird identified as a male House Finch. I have to admit, I'm a chowderhead when it comes to identifying birds. I continually confuse the Red-breasted

Nuthatch with the White-breasted Nuthatch. Like I said, I'll never remember their names but I love the distinct colors, and that's what attracts me to them.

The Northern Cardinal and the Blue Jay are the most common birds frequenting my backyard. I'll never get tired of admiring their unique, sharp, and delightful plume. There's a battle going on in my heart over my favorite bird— I guess you figured it out, it's between the Cardinal and Blue Jay, and I'm not talking baseball teams. The rich colors of these two birds sometimes bring tears to my eyes. Remember, we've gone over this, and we'll pretend, tough guys never let water trickle down from their eyes.

According to Tekiela, the scientific name for the Blue Jay is "Cyanocitta cristata." Through the lenses of my field glasses I saw a mid-sized bird with varying shades of blue and patches of black running along its back. Standing motionless, adorned with a blue crown, black collar, gray-white chest, and black hash marks on its wings, the proud bird had a soldier's bearing. To me, I saw the Blue Jay standing atop my shed as a noble bird.

Here's my challenge, the battle of colors. The Northern Cardinals (Cardinalis cardinalis) have an unmistakable color difference between the female and male. I love how the coordinating shades of brown and red distinguishes the sexes. Nature has provided us with two beautiful birds that seem to make mating spontaneous and uncomplicated. Hah, if that were the case, Rachael and I would be walking arm in arm.

I'm struck by Stan Tekiela's description of the female as, "Buff brown with tinges of red on crest and wings, a black mask and large red bill." With their combination of seductive colors and poise, I'm reminded of the eloquence of a Spanish flamenco dancer. How mysterious is that?

When I sighted a male cardinal through my binoculars I saw a bird dressed in the red coat of the Queen's Guard. Its face concealed by a black, Zorro type mask. Spots of brown and black streamed across its wings and tail. Standing astride the birdbath, I saw the brilliant red of the male cardinal as a power bird. The battle in my heart over my favorite bird rages on—cardinal versus blue jay, but the winner of the color is the "Buff brown" hen.

The rest of the day played out as expected, the library in the afternoon, Mad Dawg's early evening, then home with the pooch. Before I hit the sack, I thought I'd tell you a little bit about myself.

For the record, I'm definitely old school, as if you haven't guessed. I try to be courteous and polite even when it's hard, speak up for good people when they're being attacked, and do it (whatever the task) right the first time. For you ladies, I hold doors, pay for the date, and stand whenever you enter the room.

I shave every day, keep my hair short, and now stylish with regular appointments to see Sarah. I don't have any tattoos, but after twenty years in the Navy, I say, "Whatever floats your boat." I love to read history, travel, and do my best to avoid politics. However, I was truly moved watching the funeral service for George H. W. Bush.

This isn't a political statement, but you have to admire the forty-first president of the United States. Full disclosure, I got to meet the man, and I liked him. He died on 30 November 2018. I remember watching the memorial services for him and reading how he lived his life. He subscribed to these basic principles according to his friends and family: temperance, self-restraint, plain speaking, honesty, duty, forbearance, humility, prudence, and courage. In retrospect, this sort of represents the principles I subscribed to as I rose-up in the ranks. And, in all honesty, I can't claim to have lived them to the same extent as the forty-first.

As a history buff and a Navy man I've always been inspired by the lyrics to *Eternal Father, Strong to Save,*" written by William Whiting in 1860, and beautifully played at the funeral of President Bush. Whiting was inspired by the dangers of the sea as described in Psalm 107. Having spent so much time in tumultuous waters, I'm influenced more by the reality of the dangers of the sea. I thought I would share the lyrics with you, and let you enjoy the sweet sound of the words. Take it from me, the more you listen and hear each verse, the more you'll cherish the poetic lines. You don't need to be a sailor in order to be moved, you just need a little humility. I always find it best to read these somber words out loud and let the sound bring the hymn to life.

*Eternal Father, strong to save*
*Whose arm hath bound the restless wave*
*Who biddest the mighty ocean deep*
*It's own appointed limits keep*
*Oh, hear us when we cry to Thee*
*For those in peril on the sea*


*O Christ! Whose voices the waters heard*
*And hushed their raging at Thy Word*
*Who walked on the foaming deep*
*And calm amidst its rage didst sleep*
*Oh, hear us when we cry to Thee*
*For those in peril on the sea*

*Most Holy Sprit! Who didst brood*
*Upon the chaos dark and rude*
*And bid its angry tumult cease*
*And give, for wild confusion, peace*
*Oh, hear us when we cry to Thee*
*For those in peril on the sea*

*O Trinity of love and power*
*Our family shield in dangers hour*
*From rock and tempest, fire and foe*
*Protect us wheresoever we go*
*Thus evermore shall rise to Thee*
*Glad hymns of praise from land and sea*

Man, how does the music of this poetry not move you? Regardless of your politics, George H. W. Bush was a hell-of-a-guy, from a great generation of men and women. What, you think this tough guy cried watching the forty-first's funeral service? Like you don't know, I bawled like a baby. You could've loved the man, even though you didn't know him.

*

Well back to business. When I awoke on Sunday the Thirtieth, I was facing a bright, relatively warm December day. I needed gas for the Ridgeline and decided to head over to Harwich, fuel up, and bust Marco's you-know-what. It was also time for a long, slow run on the Cape Cod Rail Trail. I love leaving from Harwich and running toward Chatham. It's a much more tranquil area to begin your excursion into the woods. The locals tell me this section of the trail is relatively quiet, even at the height of the tourist season.

While getting gas at Speed-A-Way, Marco and I had a good friendly row. I love bantering with him. He's quick witted, funny, and I'm no match for this good looking navy man. If we were boxing, I think I'd go down in the second round, maybe the first. Okay, you may be wondering why I go all the way to Harwich for gas. Here's my reasons I love my truck and love to drive, so heading over to Harwich is a simple pleasure, occasionally to run the rail trail, and most of all, my budding friendship with Marco.

After getting gas, I parked the truck at Brooks Park and headed out on my trek. Every time I traverse the Cape Cod Rail Trail, I think of a quote by John Muir, "Come to the woods for there is rest." I love the truth of his words. Surrounded by trees gives me a feeling of being transposed back to my youth, when life was simple and straightforward. The movement of my body eases what's complicating my mind. When the run is completed, regardless of the distance covered, I am at rest.

John Muir is known as the father of the National Parks. He was an environmental publisher, naturalist, and advocate for the preservation of the wilderness. His legacy continues to be shared by millions of people from across the world. How cool is his contribution to our great country?

I had once read *Cape Cod*, by Henry David Thoreau and came across his quote depicting Cape Cod as, "A torn and thread bare garment." As much as I loved the book, I don't agree with his description of the Cape. My journey along much of Thoreau's route has taken me through dunes with hundreds of vascular flora, patches of green vegetation, brownish beach heather, low lying cranberry bogs surrounded by crevices and nooks. The sandy coast, rather than torn and bare, is sometimes shaded by clusters of woodlands, with wind, worn pitch and scrub pines. The sandy beach is often littered with large smooth and jaded boulders visible at low tide. I find the Cape an authentic reminder of those who first settled on our unique and rugged soil.

When I run the Cape Cod Rail Trail, I experience the way John Muir felt about the restfulness of the woods. For me, entering a forest is like entering a magical place. The only sounds you hear are nature's chimes. There is the temperate harmony of a breeze rustling leaves, the tiptoeing of small animals, and birds chirping in their own unique, musical language.

The paved trail is sprinkled with small, rolling hills, lined by native trees that provide a shaded gateway as you traverse through the woodland. Rays of sunlight peek through branches of deep-green pine needles creating a warm blanket during the winter months.

The view of marshes, breathtaking lakes, and cranberry bogs enhance the natural imagery that abuts the trail. During my many journeys through the wooded Garden of Eden, I've watched the flooding and harvesting of cranberries. An ocean of brilliant red rises to the surface of the water as berries break from the vine. My eyes transfixed on the coordinating colors. The clear blue sky, the early autumn foliage of russet, and the sea of red resting on slate colored water takes my breath away.

The trail is rich in vegetation and wildlife. I've seen red tail hawks soaring, bald eagles nesting, white swans floating, and numerous other colorful birds. A hawk in flight pursued by sparrow sized birds, as if in a contest fraught with gamesmanship, is a sight to see. My run came to a halt one day as I watched an eastern box turtle, with its artistically designed shell of multi-colors, waddle across the trail. One cool afternoon, I ran into a big buck, and he didn't look too happy to see me, as he escorted and protected his doe and fawns. This sailor boy knew what to do, and it wasn't in the words of Admiral James Farragut, "'Damn the torpedoes, full speed ahead."

As you run the trail or walk, you weave your way through a variety of trees and plants indigenous of the Cape. There you're shrouded by eastern red cedar, pitch pines, and black and white oaks. On many a day I'm a solitary voyager. My only company on the trail is the wind rustling the trees, the sight of nature's scenery, and the aroma of flowers, soil, and vegetation.

You don't need to be a runner to enjoy the woods. I admire the walkers, they're following Socrates advice, "Walking is man's best medicine." By now you know, I'm a quote catcher. I've maintained a diary with quotes I'd picked up during my twenty years in the Navy, and when I come across something interesting, I write it down. Some people say I'm living by clichés, but that's alright with me—I'm quoting Socrates, Thoreau, and Muir; not a bad lineup.

After enjoying my morning on the Cape Cod Rail Trail, I arrived back at the home front, made lunch, and played with Sailor. I took a siesta, unusual for me, and when I awoke, I cleaned the house and made dinner. I decided to hang-out at the home front and let the little tyke snuggle up to me. We lounged on the couch with Sailor's head resting on my thigh. The fireplace was burning with a reddish, yellow flame. I was thankful for the afternoon nap, as my eyes started to droop while researching the Catholic Faith during the 1860s.

Based upon the articles I read, the Irish population during the 1860s was approximately fifty-six percent. The vast majority of these early settlers were Catholic. I learned that Irish immigrants built Saint Peter's Church in the Town of Sandwich. A newly ordained priest began celebrating mass at the new parish in 1829. There was also supporting documentation that Catholic Services began in Harwich in 1865. My readings confirmed there were two locations, about twenty-five miles apart, for Catholics to worship.

All the work I'd done up to this point provided little in the way of acquiring information relevant to the Hartley's. The one factual thing I knew, the gale of 1869 had devastated the Mid-Cape area, and particularly, the small farming population—as evidenced by the destruction of the Hartley Farm.

The next day was New Year's Eve, and the library was scheduled to close at four o'clock. My plan was to spend the morning there focusing on the Hartley Farm, The Old Man, and Mary. Mr. Wood's poetic words were playing in my ears like a recoding, "Many a sorrow has died from remembrance." It was a simple reminder to never forget the Saxby Gale or give up finding what remains of Mary Hartley. I'm motivated and committed—I just need to know everything I can about the Hartleys and their farm.

\*

Man, I love Cape Cod in the winter. The snow is usually light, but the locals tell me the weather is unpredictable and some snow storms can "Kick your ass," their words not mine. For the most part, the weather has been moderate, but we've had our share of cold, breathtaking days.

The thirty-first of December was one of those days with a strong, warm sun, crisp air, and the clarity of an inspiring, bright-blue sky. Stepping outdoors and into a trifecta of perfect winter weather was like a summer dive into the cold waves of Nantucket Sound. My fact-finding was going well and I was in a hurry to get to the library. I figured, wrap-up my research by noon, go for an early afternoon run, and then hang with my little buddy until he was tuckered out. The day would conclude with the celebration planned at the Mad Dawg Pub. I know what you're thinking, but you're wrong. This dude planned to use Uber New Year's Eve—no DUI for this sailor.

My morning at the library was relatively productive (in other words, I didn't get much accomplished). I cut myself some slack since we were closing out 2018. After taking care of Sailor at noon, I headed over to West Dennis Beach. The wind off of Nantucket Sound was crisp and cold, yet tolerable. As usual, the parking lot was occupied with walkers and runners. These health enthusiasts were taking advantage of the moderate December weather. I ran three miles and walked the last loop for another mile. The brisk breeze off the water reddened my cheeks, the same sensation I felt standing on the ship's deck during an Atlantic crossing. The hay colored seagrass of the salt marsh was flowing in rhythm with the rippling surf of the Bass River. The sand flats along the western shore this winter day were as bleak as Thoreau's quote, "Torn and thread bare," but to me, beautiful, clothed in its temporal winter ruggedness. All of this asymmetry encapsulated under a cloudless, blue heaven combined to create a symmetry of rhapsody.

When I returned to the house it was around four in the afternoon. I chowed down a light lunch and took Sailor outdoors to frolic in the blustery air. While getting ready for my New Year's Eve night out, I realized the week's work of probing, investigating, and trying to uncover the Hartley mystery made celebrating the year end countdown as mundane as viewing reruns of *The Blair Witch Project*. My mind was definitely not on watching the euphoria of the big, "Ball Drop."

I was still focused on the blank slate my morning research produced. One of the librarians had found an obscure pamphlet containing statistical, agricultural data. The material presented in the document confirmed that in the 1860s, agricultural employment accounted for approximately twenty percent. Based upon census data, there were roughly seven hundred people employed in farming. The small number of farm workers translated into a smaller number of farms. I was impatient to learn more and New Year's Eve was a distraction. I was convinced there had to be property maps or plot plans from the 1860s archived somewhere. All of my optimism made me believe I would soon learn more about the Hartley Farm, its boundaries, and the location of the buildings. However, it didn't take long to realize how wrong I was in my prediction. I was disappointed, but not undiminished. When I came to a dead end, the librarian came to my rescue, referring me to the town hall. He recommended I make inquiries at the assessor's office, planning division, and the building department. Unfortunately, the town hall was closed on New Year's Day. There was nothing more to do until the local government reopened for business. The second of January 2019 loomed large while I waited impatiently to learn more.

In the end, as you probably suspected, I pretty much blew-off New Year's Eve. I narrowly avoided those imbibing cheap alcohol and making shallow toasts. After one Bud at Bunny's, I offered up an excuse to leave, fought off the resistance, and managed to escape. I got home to Sailor by eight o'clock. In no time, I had the fireplace roaring and Herman Wouk's, *War and Remembrance* in my hands. All and all, it turned out to be a pretty good first New Year's Eve on Cape Cod for me and my first mate.

The second of January was biting with soft, white, floating snowflakes parachuting to the ground. My eagerness to continue my research was all the warmth I needed to ward off the cold. I arrived early at the town hall and was the first to wish the blurry eyed staff a "Happy New Year!" The beauty of a small community is most of the people working in local government are friendly, helpful, and provide top notch service. Unfortunately, despite their assistance, it was strike one at the assessor's office, strike two at the planning division, and, you guessed it, strike three at the building department. Like my high school batting average, I was beginning to think the Hartley farm was an enigma, a blank page; almost as if it never existed.

I left the town hall thwarted but still determined. I'm convinced Mary Hartley will have her Christian burial, and the victims of the Saxby Gale will not be forgotten. While my research provided solid background information about the1860s, there was a lack of concrete evidence supporting the possibility of finding Mary Hartley's remains. However, her letter was the one powerful incentive that would peak even a skeptic's interest in trying to solve this mystery.

It was nearly time to share the letter and my research with Rachael and Kitten. For me, It was a "moment of truth." Have I been on a "wild goose chase?" or will they believe there's a way to honor Mary Hartley's request. If there is one thing I'd learned about problem solving, it's you often have to step back from your hypothesis and get an independent evaluation. This process helps you gain a better perspective. When you return to your theory, you need to reexamine your analysis and approach the subject with an open mind. Lucky for me, Rachael and Kitten were two aces I could rely on for an honest appraisal. I'm looking forward to hearing their thoughts and opinions.

Right before heading into the library to talk with Rachael I made and about-face. This sailor decided to wait until the seventh to approach Rachael for help. My excuse, and this was only half true, she was just getting back from vacation and needed time to settle in at work. The full, metaphorical, truth was my feet were as frosty as ice. This timid Navy Man wanted a few more days to build up enough nerve before approaching Rachael, and the additional time gave me an opportunity to gain some much needed confidence. I took full advantage of the delay, playing with the Sailor, listening to *Gonna Fly Now* the *Rocky* theme song, running, and listening to *Gonna Fly Now* the *Rocky* theme song. I know, I wrote it twice, just trying to TKO my anxiety and shyness—you get my drift.

When the big day finally arrived the *Rocky* beat, "Dah, dun, tha, dah—dah, dun, tha, dah," was ringing in my head. Okay, I'm no lyricist, but my confidence was booming. I waited until eleven in the morning to approach Rachael. I have to admit (as if you don't know me by now), I'm as scared as a high school kid trying to ask a girl to a dance. I can't even remember if the melody goes "Dah, tha, dah, or dun, dah, doo."

Rachael didn't show her usual welcoming smile when she saw me. Her look was serious and all business. After I managed to say, "Good Morning," she pretty much scolded me and said, "You shouldn't have bought me such an expensive gift."

There was no sense trying to BS her, she's a book expert. When I responded and said, "It was actually a down payment on helping me solve a mystery," Rachael eyed me suspiciously. I then presented my investigative folder to her; before she took it, she looked at me closely, sizing me up for the first time since I'd met her. As Rachael read Mary Hartley's letter and reviewed my research notes I could see a change in her demeanor. She went from evaluating and classifying my information from the perspective of a librarian, to assessing its credibility as an FBI analyst.

After Rachael reread the packet of material I'd handed her, she said, "Intriguing, would you mind if I held onto the folder for a couple of days?"

I readily agreed to her request. Rachael promised to return my material, and let me know if she would help, after she carefully reviewed my documents.

The wait to hear from Rachael was agonizing. I'm smitten with her and she's clearly an overreach on my part, but it's more than that. Rachael has an aura of friendliness that she balances with a professional's demeanor. All the library patrons seem to migrate to her and she treats everyone courteously, but with the same subtle distance. The Hartley mystery may be the key to closing that space and unlocking each other's heart.

Okay, I get it, I'm starting to sound like the end of an old, forty-five RPM whirling around on a record player. But love's a funny thing—I went from being a modest, rational guy to an irrational high school freshman attracted to the senior homecoming queen. To make matters worse, I felt I'd crossed the line by buying her an expensive gift. She knew immediately how much the books sold for, and obviously wasn't happy.

When Rachael called to tell me she was in and willing to help in my quest, my heart went flat line and my tongue was tied up in a reef knot. With some difficulty, I loosened the knot and freed my tongue enough to thank her. Rachael asked, "Michael, are you okay?" A little white lie popped out of my mouth and I mumbled something about the dentist. Somehow, despite my verbal deficiency, we managed to arrange a meeting at the library late the next morning.

When I awoke, I busied myself until nine-thirty; then, watched the clock tic, tic, tic as if time were a slow moving snail. I had an irrational fear the minutes would stand still, and eleven o'clock would never come.

# 3

When Rachael and I met at eleven o'clock, her smile and friendliness had returned. I got a clear indication she understood the serious commitment I'd made to solving the mystery of Mary Hartley's death. Rachael agreed we should pick Kitten's brain since she's a well-known local and real estate agent with contacts who may be helpful.

Rachael was as impressed as I was with Mary Hartley's ability to write an articulate letter under extreme conditions. Her foresight to preserve it in a Mason jar was heroic. Mary didn't panic, she chronicled the events as she saw them, and made her plea for a Christian burial. What an amazing woman!

Rachael had read my notes and the remarks I'd written in the margins of the documents I'd prepared. I had jotted down passionate words expressing a commitment to *"Never give up the search for Mary Hartley."* In bold letters, I wrote, ***"I promise to give Mary a proper burial."*** I also expressed myself emphatically; *"I will never forget the victims of the Saxby Gale."*

Unlike me, Rachael approached the problem with the professionalism of an FBI analyst. She simply looked at the facts; her focus wasn't emotional like mine. She encouraged me to keep researching the small population of farmers and limited number of people employed in farming. She believed this information may lead us to documents that could facilitate our search.

Listening to Rachael, my optimism and excitement increased. I was now working with a trained professional, and that expert was Rachael Morgan. What a cool partnership for a thirty-eight-year-old, lovestruck schoolboy like me.

Rachael rode with me as we headed over to Kitten's, and I couldn't help thinking how natural she looked sitting beside me in my truck. I pressed the image permanently in my mind and wished for more days with Rachael at my side.

Meeting us on her front porch, Kitten was her usual, jovial self. I introduced her to Rachael and the two exchanged pleasantries. Seeing me with a stunning beauty, Kitten winked at me when Rachael wasn't looking. This twenty-year Navy veteran blushed like a sixteen-year-old. Kitten couldn't help but laugh at me; leaving Rachael with a quizzical look on her face.

When we finally got down to business Kitten was as intrigued as we were. She listened to my presentation and took the time to slowly review my notes. She was zoned in as she digested all of my material. Kitten then reread Mary Hartley's letter with intensity. This was the first time I'd seen her with a seriousness of purpose. You could tell hidden behind her satirical humor and banter is a very smart woman.

As she looked up from reading the documents, she spoke very deliberately and said, "I've sold a lot of properties on the land where the old farm once stood, and I've always had an interest in its history, but I could never learn much. My guess is shortly after the Saxby Gale passed the land was promptly broken up into parcels. Just like you wrote, people needed land to live on and with the population increasing; the Hartley Farm provided a lot of tracts for new homesteads. You can only imagine the shenanigans that occurred in 1869. The Hartleys probably had no heirs or relatives, and the powers to be took little time dividing up the profits on the sale of the much-needed land. When you look at some of the beautiful houses lining the Old King's Highway, you can kind of get the picture."

Rachael was quick to respond and asked, "Based upon your experience as a realtor, do you have any suggestions of where we might possibly find information relating to the Hartley Farm?"

"My friend Jane at the Historical Society may be able to help you; I'll give her a call if you want to head over there now."

"Thank you, it will be a great help to speak with her," responded Rachael.

I felt like a spectator listening to these two smart women communicate with each other. That was cool with me; I was working shoulder-to-shoulder with Rachael to solve a mystery and was silently singing like a lark.

Okay, I was even happier with Rachael back in the passenger seat of my truck. The radio was on with Cape Country playing softly in the background. Rachael and I shared our thoughts, but mostly we remained quiet; me stealing gazes at the woman of my dreams.

Jane at the Historical Society was expecting us and happy to help. Within minutes of meeting her, she dropped the biggest surprise on us since the discovery of Mary Hartley's letter. Jane casually mentioned the existence of a painting that accurately depicted the physical layout of the Hartley farm. She explained, society members had done extensive research in order to acquire greater knowledge of the Hartley Farm and its historical importance to the Town of Dennis. It was during their inquiry that they came across what they believed, was a copy of the original Hartley Farm painting.

"It was very unusual for such a prominent piece of property to be absent of any physical records, filings, or plot plans. Over the years there had been title problems with a number of house sales on the old Hartley farm property, but the issues always seemed to get resolved.

"I remember the excitement our members felt when they were informed there was a painting of the Hartley Farm in a gallery on Route 6A. We were all told, it was a beautifully, captured, artistic rendition titled, *The Hartley Farm*. The painting was described as a map of the property, and very expensive. Still, our members discussed purchasing it as part of our historical preservation campaign. When I went to the gallery to inquire, I'd been told by neighbors it had closed and the painting was sold to another dealer, possibly on 6A."

Rachael and I looked at each other with an aura of excitement. I was preoccupied with what the existence of an accurate portrayal of the farm could mean to our investigation. A knowledge of the physical location of the house, barn, shed, and boundaries greatly increased the probability of finding Mary Hartley's remains. While I was consumed by these thoughts, Rachael took the lead in questioning Jane.

"Do you have the name of the Gallery where the painting had been for sale?"

"Yes, I do, the Rose Gallery in Eastham."

"Do you have the name of the owner," asked Rachael.

"I believe her first name was Rose, she was well into her eighties when her shop closed. It was a small gallery in a renovated garage. Through the grapevine, I'd heard she passed away; people told me she was a sweet woman with a passion for the arts," responded Jane.

"And you mentioned the painting was expensive?" asked Rachael.

"Yes, that's what I'd heard, it wasn't a painting most likely to be sold. Gallery owners have a tendency to showcase one or two prestigious and expensive paintings with little hope of selling them. The idea is it enhances their art collection and often times facilitates a sale of a less expensive piece. I suspect whoever bought the painting was a friend and paid a fair price to help Rose out."

"Why do you think the painting is still on the Cape and hasn't been sold?" asked Rachael.

"Well we made some further inquiries without much luck. But when I'd heard about the painting, it was selling for ten thousand dollars. I can't imagine the cost today, or who would pay such a steep price for a rendition of the Hartley Farm."

Before Rachael could answer, I said, "I would, I'm very much interested in the painting, and I have the perfect place for it in my new home. It would be fitting, since my small piece of the Cape sits in the middle of the Hartley Farm."

Both Rachael and Jane looked at me with astonishment. I don't have a tendency to show off my wealth; I'm sure it's a topic you'll become more aware of as my story unfolds. For now, you should know I'm a jeans and a tee-shirt, khakis and button-down shirt sort of guy, boat shoes, sneakers; thrifty and modest in my spending.

Rachael promptly regained her composure and thanked Jane. I also extended my appreciation for her help. Jane responded and said, "Don't be discouraged. I'm sure a lovely couple like you will find the painting if it's still on the Cape. If you do locate it, I would love to see it and maybe photograph it for the Historical Society. We can pay you a small amount to help cover the cost of the panting."

This time Rachael differed to me, and I felt like we were part of the same team. I responded to Jane and said, "When we find the painting, and we will, you'll be the first to be notified and you can take all the pictures you need. I'll also make the painting available at your request. The residents should get to enjoy a beautiful painting, and an important piece of Dennis' history."

"Well, I very much look forward to hearing from you," said Jane.

Rachael and I again thanked Jane profusely. She not only gave us a potential lead, but more importantly, hope. At this point in our investigation I hadn't considered that the original painting Mrs. Murphy described could be related to the one hanging in the Rose Gallery. It was a dot I hadn't yet connected.

When we got outside, Rachael, with her analyst hat-on eyed me with suspicion and remained silent until we got into my truck. Once behind the wheel of the 2018 Honda Ridgeline, Rachael said, "A pricey first edition book signed by the author and a commitment to purchase an expensive painting. What's your story, Michael Maine?"

"Rachael, my story's boring. I'm a twenty-year veteran of the United States Navy with a reasonably good pension."

"And?"

"Well, I've never been excessive with my money, I've saved and invested wisely over the past twenty years."

I paused as Rachael watched me intently. She didn't respond, her penetrating gaze told me she was trying to figure me out. I didn't think she was being intrusive, but I did get a sense she knew I was holding my story close to my heart, and it wasn't simply the money.

When I continued, I said, "I'm fortunate to have financial security, and the money to purchase a painting with historical value. It will also serve as a reminder of Mary Hartley and the Saxby Gale. Your gift, well, I couldn't resist buying the two books for you at Christmas, because... I consider you one of the two or three friends friends I have on the Cape. My motive was simply a gesture of thanks for all the help you've given me at the library."

"Well Mr. Money, eventually you'll tell me your whole story, but for now, why don't I treat you to a coffee and we can discuss a plan to go forward."

Rachael was smiling and I couldn't help but smile back, and with pleasure said, "I accept the date for our second business meeting."

"Just so you know Mr. frugal Sailor Boy, I'm picking up the tab for the coffee, but if you want something to eat, it's a Dutch Treat."

"I accept your conditions, partner."

We headed over to the double Ds at the Colonial Square Mall. Most of the tables were empty, so we grabbed a corner one to discuss our strategy. Rachael sat quietly as I relayed my earlier visit with Mrs. Murphy, the great-granddaughter of Rose Flynn. I had casually mentioned the coincidence of the two women named Rose (Rose Flynn and the gallery Rose), and the missing original Hartley Farm painting, but hadn't paid much attention to it at the time. Rachael took in what I'd said with the concentration of an analyst filing and storing information for possible later use.

I had to admire Rachael and how she communicated with Jane. She had her talking freely and, in the end, Jane provided valuable information. Rachael was so cool she didn't respond when Jane mentioned us being a couple. Unlike me, my heart skipped a beat or two, maybe even three. Hey, I'm head over heels for Rachael and completely over-invested in the sentimental side of the investigation. That's why I needed her analytical mind if we're going to find the Hartley Farm painting and solve this mystery.

The emotional roller coaster I'd been on was very unlike me. I think being retired from the Navy and traveling across the country caused me to reflect on my past. Clearly, I had become much more sensitive and mushy. While I would have loved to forge a life with Rachael and maybe even start a family, I was not lonely for companionship. While in the Navy, I learned how to develop short-term friendships and I've maintained the ability on the Cape. My small circle includes Kitten, Marco, Ed from the Yellow Cottage, and some of the regulars that hang out at the pubs. And by now, you know I'm sort of a homebody who enjoys hanging out with his mate, Sailor. But I know a compelling change had come over me and it wasn't only Rachael. I believe Mary Hartley was trying to speak directly to me. In my dreams and in my heart, I had a strange longing to be consumed by her ghost. I believed our spiritual connection was the way to locate her remains and give her a Christian burial. Mr.

Woods poem, *The Saxby Gale,* is a reminder that we all have an obligation to never forget the victims of tragic events.

Rachael is amazing, without hesitation she committed to doing all she could to help me locate the Hartley painting. Even though she believes the key to solving our puzzle was too find it, I detected a subtle skepticism in her. At the same time, Rachael showed an obvious excitement in participating in the search. In the deep recesses of my heart, I was hoping there could be more to our relationship than simply our investigation.

Rachael recommended we start canvassing the galleries after the February school vacation. She was busy at the library preparing programs to keep the local kids occupied during their holiday week. She also knew from living on the Cape, most of the galleries would still be shut down during the off-season or have limited hours. I was thrilled when Rachael suggested I frequent the library more often, especially on days when she was working. It was an opportunity for her to assist me digging through their archives. She thought there was a chance we would find information of value amongst the newspaper clippings and old records.

When I dropped Rachael off at her house, she exposed her beautiful white teeth with a smile and thanked me for a wonderful day. She told me she very much enjoyed being a librarian, but she said, "I have to admit, I've always loved the hunt to find important information needed in an investigation."

After Rachael closed the door to my truck, I knew one thing, it was time to head home and go for a long, hard run. My emotions were surging; the fruity scent of Rachael permeated the air. The physical attraction was strong, I had fought the urge to embrace her. While I freely admit her beauty is undeniable, it's her brain that is second to none, and I greatly admired her intelligence. She also has a cool, gracious way when dealing with people. She gets them to lighten up and openly engage in conversation. They immediately become helpful, revealing more than they thought they knew. I shivered when I thought of her ability to obtain information, and how long it would be before she knew my story, a tale I've kept bottled up for twenty years.

\*

Back at the ranch, I took Sailor out for a little physical activity. I was amazed how quickly he's responded to his training. Most of all, this loveable pup has become family to me, and I can't wait to spend time with him. With the tuckered-out little critter sleeping on the sofa, I headed out on a run and immediately broke my cardinal rule. I'm a three-to-four mile runner who likes to walk the same distance on the way home; and to use a long worn out cliché, "smell the roses."

After spending a wonderful day with Rachael, my hormones could be used for rocket fuel, and I couldn't control my legs or my body. I ran a hard eight miles and even though I broke my training rule, I felt fantastic. I've maintained a simple exercise program for twenty years, and it's based on four principles: flexibility, core, strength, and cardio. Running eight miles is not part of the agenda, but for the love of Rachael, I'd do a marathon. I'm more than smitten with her; I'm in love. I know I need to be patient and not try to overreach. With a bundle of luck, maybe she'll see qualities in me worth pursuing. A modest guy like me can only hope.

Okay, enough of this schmaltzy stuff; it was time to grab a bite to eat, so I headed over to the Mad Dawg Pub. The place was surprisingly crowded, but I managed to get a seat at the bar. I had a delicious fish dinner accompanied by two cold, invigorating Buds. I almost asked for a third, but rules are rules and my limit's two. I returned home by nine thirty, lazed around with Sailor as he snuggled at my feet. I thought I'd finish reading *Dangerous Ambition* before I hit the sack. I figured it would be nice to discuss a book with Rachael that she had a passion for and enjoyed. Unfortunately, while reading, I had occasionally lost my concentration. My mind wandered with thoughts of the library, where I would sneak peeks at my girl. At least Rachael was my girl in my heart.

The next morning, guess who woke me up with the rising sun? My four-legged roommate was now my alarm clock without the snooze button. I wrestled with the hound in my bed to give him a little love. After getting up, I took care of my usual chores, and headed to Cold Storage in East Dennis to walk the beach. On a clear day you can look out across the bay and see a pencil line sketch of the coast, from Eastham to Provincetown. Low tide was at eight in the morning, plenty of time to get my exercise in before the waves brushed up against the soft sand. The weather was icicle cold with a strong biting wind off Cape Cod Bay. The sky had a ferocious dirty-gray color full of nimbus clouds. The threat overhead had the angry look of a monstrous horror movie, as if the darkest cloud patches were a black hole pulling you toward the mouth of "Godzilla" about to consume you. It was the type of day I readily embraced. Each step I took beat in harmony with the music of the crashing surf. It was a tempo that kept my 180 pound body moving along the shore. While the bite of the wind had left my face with the sting of a burn, it was the sweet sensation of being alive.

I started from the jetty at Cold Storage and headed out toward Quivett Neck. I usually never make it all the way. There's a series of large rocks, like crumbled remains of the Temple of Dagon, exposed at low tide offering a great place to hang out. It takes me a good thirty minutes to get there and thirty minutes to get back to the jetty. The walk has its challenges, I'm either a poor example of a ballet dancer performing a ciseaux over tide pools, or a hiker in ski boots chugging across the soft sand. When I reach the stone fortress, I like to sit and stare out into the bay. I love the sound of the ocean, and the sight of white foam atop of the crashing waves. Even on a cold winter's day there's usually a pioneering seagull hunting for a meal. Like a sleuth in the night, the feathered bandit braves the elements diving into the frigid water and retrieving its reward.

I love the sight of seagulls in flight, especially the lone bird soaring along the horizon. There's an independence and creativity captured in the grace of a solitary bird challenging the aerodynamics of flight. For the ground-bonded spectator the daring, feathered friend's artful maneuvers look effortless.

When I returned home I took a warm shower, ate a quick lunch, and headed over to the library. Rachael was juggling her duties; I hardly saw her. To stay occupied, I started to make a list of all the galleries from Eastham to Sandwich. I knew many of the galleries would be closed for the season, so I figured, I'm really wasting my time writing down the name of galleries.

The better approach was to get started right away, drive Route 6A, and visit the open galleries. We could start in Eastham where the Rose Gallery was located and work our way back through Orleans, Brewster, Dennis, Yarmouth, Barnstable, and Sandwich. When we encountered a closed one, we could note it for a return visit. There's a redundancy built into this method which, normally, isn't a good thing. But Rachael works a full-time job and has limited time to travel around searching for a painting. I roughly calculated to visit all the galleries on 6A when she was available, would probably take us until September. My dilemma was whether to do some of the inquiries on my own or wait for Rachael. I decided it was best to begin the search together. We had quickly become a team, and like most teams, we brought different skills to the table. Rachael was superb at obtaining and evaluating information. Her analytical process offset my emotional approach to our investigation. There was also the matter of the hefty price tag for the Hartley painting. Based upon what we'd been told, it was probably too costly for most buyers. I also agreed with Jane's assessment, the painting was most likely used to grab the attention of customers with the hope they would buy something less expensive. The real reason I wanted to wait for Rachael (as if you didn't know), was the opportunity for her to look into my heart and see the type of man I truly am, and however long it takes, hopefully she would fall in love with me.

After abandoning my list making I started to nod off. I was about to enter the dream stage when Rachael came up behind me and said, "Sleepy head, you're already slacking."

I almost fell off my chair as Rachael dropped a stack of files on my desk jolting me from my slumber. She mentioned she was way too busy to talk but came across a bundle of files in the basement of the library dated 1850 to 1900. The tower of old files sitting in front of me tilted to the right and resembled the Leaning Tower of Pisa. Needless to say, there were a ton of documents and articles cut from newspapers to read. Rachael said, "Going through the files is a long shot, but it may be worth the effort." Instantly, she disappeared; no stealing quick looks at her when she's working behind closed doors. No wonder I fell asleep.

I headed over to double Ds, bought a large coffee, and with a renewed energy plowed through the material. Two hours later I came across a newspaper notice without a date that read, "Hartley property to be sold in small parcels will take place on Saturday as scheduled."

The vague notice appeared to confirm what Kitten had believed. She hit the nail on the head when she had intimated the land was swiftly organized into individual parcels. People needed a place to live and farm, so no one asked any questions. Kitten thought there probably weren't any heirs to the estate and the powers-that-be took full advantage. They discreetly broke up the land into housing lots and sold them to an apathetic public. The lack of historical property documents suggested shenanigans took place in the breakup of the Hartley Farm.

Once again, I was impressed with Kitten's insight. The four-by-four inch notice I'd discovered told us more than the article suggested. What was clear, the painting now looked to be our only hope of locating the remains of Mary Hartley.

When Rachael finally surfaced, I showed her my rough draft of the plan to begin our search and the newspaper clipping. She thought the plan was a methodical approach rather than a random, helter-skelter search. Rachael agreed with me, finding the painting was the key to learning more about the physical structure of the farm and our best chance of locating Mary Hartley.

Rachael cautioned me and said, "We need to be patient, it may take time to locate the painting. Believe me, I'm committed to however long it takes." She then apologized for having to delay the start of our investigation until after school vacation.

I responded and said, "If the work you do for children is important to you Rachael, it's important to me."

"Michael. Thank you."

"Rachael, we're both committed to solving this mystery, and I don't expect to walk into the first Gallery and find the painting. As the weather warms, more galleries will resume their normal business hours. If we don't find the painting right away, our chances of locating it over the spring or summer months should greatly improve. We may need to return to some of the towns we'd already visited as more galleries reopen for business. If we wait until spring, it may end up costing us potential leads. It's possible we may include the galleries in the Outer-Cape towns of Wellfleet,

Truro, and Provincetown. But for now, I believe we have a solid plan to follow."

Rachael reached out and placed her hand on my arm, smiled and said, "Michael, I'm as committed as you are to solving this mystery. I too, very much want to give Mary Hartley a Christian burial, and I'll never forget the victims of the Saxby Gale. I can commit to spending one day a week with you, and maybe two, depending on my work schedule."

Rachael paused and rather than respond directly, I nodded in agreement.

When she continued, she said, "There'll be times when I'll need to cancel because of last minute changes to my schedule, and the April school vacation is even more popular than the February one. You'll need to be patient, but remember the painting is expensive and a long shot to be sold. Even if it has been sold, there should be a record of the sale. We can approach the new owner, ask to let us at least view the painting. I'm sure the buyer, most likely an art lover, will be happy to cooperate. Now, I have to return to work, and I'm sure it's time for you to go take care of Sailor."

I tried to keep my eyes on Rachael as she spoke, but I couldn't help stealing a look at her beautiful hand resting on my arm. My high school boy's crush was embarrassing, and I pledged to never again wash the shirt I was wearing. I'm in love with Rachael, so I took her advice and said goodbye.

Back at home, I took the little critter for a walk, and decided to grill, hang at the house, and continue to read Susan Hertog's book. The twenty-sixth of February was a painfully, long way off, but Rachael was right, I needed to be patient. To be honest, I don't think I'd be able to find the painting without her.

January would have been a tough month to begin our search. The weather most often is unpredictable, and many of the small to midsize galleries stay closed until March. A few larger shops normally remain open year-round, but that can be hit or miss. So even starting at the end of February was still a bit early. Despite the challenges, visiting the open galleries was a good opportunity to facilitate our hunt for the painting. Our time wouldn't be wasted, I'd be driving around with Rachael (a fantasy come true) and progressing in our search.

To pass the days, I placed the twenty-sixth of February furthest from my thoughts. Mostly, I adhered to my normal routine. In the mornings, I played with my buddy, ran or walked when the weather permitted, and bird watched. The afternoons were spent hanging out at the library. Three or four nights a week my evenings out bounced between the

Mad Dawg Pub and Bunny's. The other nights were spent with Sailor. I was reading a book a week and greatly enjoyed the home life.

The truth be told, my afternoons spent at the library gazing at Rachael as she raced by me, smiling, giving me a quick wave and a wink, was all the incentive I needed to remain patient. I would soon have Rachael in the passenger seat of my truck one or two days a week. I'm convinced having her sitting next to me and learning about me; she would see beyond my limitations and fall in love with a man who loved her, respected her, and would be a supportive partner for life. One lovestruck sailor can only hope!

On the twenty-sixth of February, I headed over to Rachael's house. As I approached her front door she emerged wearing jeans, hiking shoes, a heavy winter sweater, gloves, and a sleeveless, down puffer vest. We exchanged good mornings as I raced to open the front passenger side door of my Ridgeline. The first thing I noticed was how relaxed and excited Rachael appeared. Her glow was as bright as the early morning sunshine and as genuine as her heart. I've watched Rachael enough over the past five months to recognize sincerity when I see it. At work, she's always friendly and supportive of the people who need assistance at the library. Her pleasant demeanor can even get a smile out of the occasional local grump.

Before I could start the truck, Rachael tossed her backpack to me and said, "I packed us lunch for our travels, and since we have a nice bright winter sun, I want to make the most of the day."

After placing Rachael's backpack on the rear seat, I turned to face her and gave her a Tom Cruise type smile showing all thirty-two teeth and said, "Thank you for making lunch, I'm on a tight budget." Pausing as we both laughed, I then said, "I'm looking forward to a full day and hopefully a productive one."

"We're facing long odds, but we have a good plan, plenty of time, and evidently, despite your tight budget, lots of money to cover the expenses of our investigation. That's why I did my part and packed us lunch; I'm on a much more restrictive budget than you." As Rachael said this she had a teasing look on her face to let me know she wasn't waiting for a response.

The traffic was light and it hadn't taken long for us to reach 6A in Dennis. We crossed over into Brewster, and as we drove by our fourth gallery it was obvious many were still shuttered for the off-season. I tried to make small talk and put a positive spin on the number of businesses still closed. I didn't want Rachael to become discouraged, and I certainly didn't want our adventure halted before we could really have a chance to get to know each other better.

Rachael immediately put me at ease when she said, "Part of the mystery is the hunt for the Hartley Farm painting, and who knows, maybe there's more than one painting or even a diary of some sort yet to be discovered. Besides, I know it's still the off-season and we'll come back this way until we're satisfied we completed a thorough search. We'll visit as many galleries as we can in the town or area we select, but the Cape is too fascinating of a place to waste the day simply looking for a painting. Since we're spending time together, I want to share as much of the natural beauty of our historic peninsula as I can with a fellow wash-ashore."

Listening to Rachael talk in such a carefree manner sent a surge through my body that made me want to propose to her on the spot. Her willingness to help me with a search that was at best, a long shot, was one thing. Her enthusiasm to share her time, and the natural beauty of the Cape with me was another matter. Maybe there was hope for this love-struck sailor after all.

Once we reached Eastham, we stopped at a handful of closed galleries and peeked through the windows to see if there were paintings of farms visibly displayed. Rachael had assumed the role of scribe, keeping notes. She wrote down the name of the business, telephone numbers, and any information helpful to our search.

A little further along 6A, we came upon a small open gallery and talked with the owner. He was new to the area, but not art. There was a crew of builders remodeling his shop. He hadn't heard of the Rose Gallery or the Hartley Painting, but told us he would keep an eye out for it. We exchanged contact information and said our goodbyes.

Our last stop was on the border of North Eastham and South Wellfleet. The sign read Gifts, Art, & Other Objects. The store had a nice display of products for sale. The art was mostly posters of beach scenes, the doors of the Cape, and boats on the water. A young woman, who looked to be in her mid-twenties, managed the store. She wasn't familiar with the Rose Gallery or the Hartley Painting. However, she had confirmed what we suspected when she said, "I majored in art history in college and someday, would love to own a gallery. I spend most of my day's off visiting the art studios and shops on the Outer-Cape. The painting you described isn't really the type you would find there. The galleries usually exhibit more contemporary themes and various scenes of the sea, landscapes, and the natural, environmental beauty of the Cape. "

It was nearly two o'clock in the afternoon by the time we left Gifts, Art, & Other Objects. On our way back to the center of Eastham, Rachael directed me to park in the lot at the Cape Cod National Seashore, home of the Salt Pond Visitor Center. Once there, she grabbed her backpack from the rear passenger seat and exited the truck. I followed her outside where the sun was bright and the air cold. Rachael dropped the tailgate and began to set out the lunch she'd prepared for us. Her menu included sandwiches, snacks, cold drinks, and a thermos with hot, strong, and black coffee.

As we sat on the tailgate eating and chatting, it was surreal to me. I wouldn't have had the courage to ask Rachael for a date, but here we were, spending the day together sharing the delightful lunch she'd prepared for the two of us. She had a joy about her that put me at ease. The fit looked as natural as a Jennifer Anderson and Adam Sandler movie. I let myself believe there was a foundation for a lasting relationship, and my hope, Rachael would desire the same as me.

My instinct was to check myself and not get too far ahead of a potential romance. Rachael appeared to be enjoying herself, and while I tried not to show it, at times, my nerves would overtake me and I thought I would say something ridiculous. When this happened, Rachael seemed to sense it, and either redirected the conversation, or offered me more food to eat or coffee to drink. She certainly had a skill for making me feel comfortable and sound interesting.

After we finished eating, Rachael said, "It's time for a little adventure before we lose the sun and it gets too cold."

"What do you have in mind?" was my lame response.

"A short hike of course." With a light elbow to my gut Rachael continued talking and said, "Only if you're up for it."

We both laughed as I faked pain and said, "Ow! I think so."

"It's a good thing, since I didn't want to carry you. This is one of my favorite places and I wanted to share it with you. I love the visitor center, the view of Salt Pond Bay, and the hiking trails that take you through the woods, marshes, and along the water."

"Lead the way, now that my pain is gone. I need to burn off a bunch of calories after the delicious lunch you prepared for us, thank you."

"My pleasure, I'm glad you enjoyed your sandwich, half of mine, and both of our snacks."

We shared another laugh at Rachael's quip; I definitely was a chowhound eating more than my share of food. To be honest, I was aware of this, but found it easier to keep eating than to converse naturally. I didn't have Rachael's gift for casual conversation, especially when my heart was racing from the simple joy of eating lunch with the woman of my dreams.

Rachael led me to the rear of the visitor center where we stood next to the two-rail fence. The wooden railing corrals the building and contains the wintery, brown undergrowth. From this vantage point, we looked out over the horizon as far as the eye could see. The view was spectacular in its natural unblemished beauty; a composition of pines and leafless trees of various sizes and forms, water rippling to the rhythm of the wind, a sky with specs of blue penetrating the cumulus clouds hanging overhead, and in the distance, a physical structure that appeared to be a rustic, old barn. A dichotomy of light and dark—old and new—blue and gray—winter browns and summer greens was spectacular.

If, only for a moment, let yourself stand in the shoes of a painter. Mounted on the easel in front of you is your blank canvas stretched over a wood frame; gesso applied; you then select a brush. Before you begin, you close your eyes and imagine the scene you're about to paint. When you open them, you're no longer standing in the cold alongside a wooden rail, but rather, in an art museum admiring a Thomas Cole landscape as water rolls down from your eyes. Suddenly, you realize it's not art that is making you emotional, but the undisguised natural beauty cascading in front of you. Nature disguised as artistry to those who see the transcendental creation surrounding them.

At that moment, I could feel the moisture in my eyes. I sensed Rachael was looking at me and saw my reaction. I stood embarrassed until I felt her hand cup mine and we silently gazed out over Salt Pond Bay.

"It's very beautiful, I often drive out here just to sketch and admire the view. For me, it never gets old, the vista may appear to be the same, but it never really is—the sun, the movement of the water, shadows, and a host of other subtle changes alter your perception; making each time you view this natural treasure a unique piece of art expressing its multiple personalities," said Rachael.

"It truly is a breathtaking view. It's a much different perspective from being on a ship patrolling the shoreline. The views from around the world are so different. I've seen the natural aesthetic of rugged terrain, rocky coasts, mountains, volcanoes, oceans of greenery, and armies of palm trees. All are truly amazing. But standing here, there's a serenity I feel just looking out across the salt pond and seeing the vastness of the Atlantic."

Rachael nudged me and said, "If you're ready, we can become part of the natural painting with a short hike around the salt pond. We still have daylight, and enough time for you to burn off those extra calories you mentioned."

Rachael led the way as we strolled past the amphitheater and down the slope behind the visitor center. We walked the dirt path along the shore. My face absorbed the hard slap of the wind jetting off the water on our right. The sky was graying as we navigated our way along the one-point-two-mile loop. The trail was easy to follow leading us in a circle back to the visitor center. The hike was truly humbling. With every step we took it was evident that our relevance was dwarfed by the largeness of the natural surroundings. I've had this same feeling many times when encircled by the seemingly sterile vastness of the ocean. But with eyes that truly see beyond the barren water, there is art. The whitecapped waves, the array of clouds, and the sun, whether descending or rising, all combine to create a compelling scene where mankind's significance is diminished by the immensity of the world.

The ride home to Dennis was serene and relatively quiet. We listened to Cape Country playing in the background. Rachael would softly sing or hum some of the songs as we traveled through Orleans and Brewster. We periodically shared our thoughts about the day and the next steps in the investigation. Neither of us mentioned Rachael holding my hand and we avoided any more physical contact the rest of the day.

When I dropped Rachael off at her house, we made plans to see each other at the library. We firmed up our next engagement for the following week so we could continue with our search. As I was driving away, a strong presence of Mary Hartley began to overtake me. Suddenly, I was overwhelmed with a desire to solve her mystery. But it became much more than my need to honor her request. I was overpowered by her presence and felt a warm feeling of love. It was as if Mary was silently communicating with me in a way that brought Rachael closer to me. It was like she was Cupid uniting us in love, and through our love, Rachael and I will solve this mystery. With this unusual sentimentality controlling me, I couldn't wait to get home. I had a compelling need to stand on my patio near the place where I'd found the Mason jar containing Mary Hartley's letter.

When I arrived at the ranch, Sailor had other ideas. I could tell he was hungry for attention. The pup showed his sentiment by jumping all over me. As I played with him, he continuously licked my face and hands. When the little tyke finally looked satisfied, he bounded toward the door, dragging me out for a nice walk. After half-a-mile, he abruptly turned toward home and pulled me like a Roman chariot. When we arrived back at the house the worn out pooch was ready to eat, so I filled his bowl and grabbed a Bud.

I put the rear spotlight on and walked outdoors to the edge of the patio. My mind wandered over the wonderful day spent with Rachael. Suddenly, a wind tunnel-like force thrust me to the exact place where I'd found the Mason jar. A puff of warmth permeated my entire body. I felt the tingle of someone lightly moving their fingers across my cheeks. Slowly, Mary's spirit closed in on me, as if she were pressed up against me in a crowded elevator. I whispered, "Where are you Mary Hartley?" A tear trickled down my check when I heard no response.

Standing in my backyard on that cold February evening, my thoughts wondered back to Rachael. She's a strong, smart, self-assured woman. Mary Hartley had these same traits. The Saxby Gale was destroying her world, while Old Man Hartley, in the face of havoc created by the storm, became unhinged. Yet, Mary had the presence to chronicle the frightful events taking place during the superstorm. She rested her hope for a Christion burial by preserving her letter in a Mason jar.

The tear rolled off my face and landed in the grass. Moments later, I could hear a faint whisper, but the words eluded me. I looked around, there was no one in the yard but me. The soft sound of a woman's voice grew to a murmur. Her words hummed with the rhythm of a canticle. I closed my eyes to a vision of Mary. With heartbreaking sadness she was chanting a short poem. Repeating the verse over and over, as if it had no beginning or end. The lyrics sang to me until I began to repeat them out loud. I felt chilled to the depths of my soul as each syllable rang out.

"When evening came, all was gone.
A gale of wind, not of laughter;
My grave unholy, cold dirt my tomb—
Why am I forgotten?"

Sailor's bark brought me back to reality and I let him out to join me. His presence was reassuring. The four words, "Why am I forgotten," played over in my mind like a broken record. Another bark from my pup made me realize tears hadn't stopped flowing down my cheeks. I wiped away the warm wetness and took a last sip of beer. Hunger and an urge for human contact overcame me. I put Sailor in the house and headed over to the Mad Dawg Pub. The restaurant was packed but I was able to grab a single seat at the bar and ordered some chow. I must have appeared distracted because one of the bartenders asked, "Hey Mike, what's up, woman problems?'

"No, Bill, nothing that interesting in this guy's life."

We talked for a while, I ate my meal and caught up on the local gossip and news. I'm really becoming an accepted regular; Bill filled me in on who's dating who, breakups, and the couple of knuckleheads who got arrested. My brain was abuzz and it wasn't from the alcohol; too much scuttlebutt wasn't my idea of a pleasant evening. After one beer, I made my escape and returned to the homestead. I arrived home before nine, spent the rest of the night with the pooch cozying up to me, the fire burning bright, and trying to concentrate on reading an old John Buchan novel, *The Power-House*. But my mind was on the haunting melody of Mary's poem and her growing supernatural presence in my life.

Unlike most nights when I make my way to bed at eleven o'clock or so, I fell into an unsettled sleep on the couch. Mary Hartley penetrated my dreams. Her hand extended from the earth—words echoing, "Help me, help me! All was gone...My unholy grave...Why am I

109

forgotten?" When I woke up, my little buddy was snuggling up against me dreaming the dreams of the unencumbered.

Crawling off the couch my body had the flexibility of a steel beam. A fog of fatigue clouded my mind as I made my way to the kitchen. My consciousness was disturbed by the unsettling dream of Mary Hartley. While drinking a mug of stronger than usual black coffee, my ears rang with the cry from an echo deep in a canyon of despair, "Help me, help me!"

Sailor nudged me, and then bounded for the door. My buddy's demands made me concentrate on our morning routine. Once completed, I thought about Rachael. I didn't want to appear eager, so I decided to avoid the library for a day or two. After the first day, I felt like a suspended high schooler missing his girlfriend. I couldn't wait to return to that warm building, laden with books, and Rachael; but I still had a small punch list of chores to complete. I'd been putting off finishing them and that didn't sit right with me, so I sucked it up and got to work.

Once my domestic duties were finished, it was time to see Sarah. My hair was looking a little long and I wanted to maintain my stylish look—for you know who. Sarah from New-Do has a great personality. She's always smiling, talking, and full of questions. When I entered her shop she must have detected a change in me. She greeted me with a seductive look and said, "Lover boy, things must be going well. Looks like you caught that 'Hail Mary pass.'" Of course, she said it loud enough for what seemed like a full-scale orchestra of ninety people gathered in the shop to hear her performance. The applause from what looked like an all women marching band was deafening to this overly embarrassed sailor. My face flushed two tones brighter than the color of Kelly LeBrock's dress in *The Woman in Red*! I babbled an unwitty response and looked for an empty chair to hide. I didn't get passed the sheepish smile that greeted my fellow patrons when Sarah said, "You're up handsome, you're about to get handsomer."

I made my way over to her chair and whispered, "Gee Sarah, I thought what was said in the salon chair stayed in the salon chair?"

"Of course it does honey, I mean, it stays in the New-Do family of gossip." Sarah got another round of clapping, laughing, and what seemed to this shrinking violet, a standing ovation from her fans.

"Now Michael, don't be embarrassed. Just tell little, old Sarah everything that's been going on in your love life?"

"Honestly, there's not much to tell. I haven't caught much yet."

111

"Yet? Something's up, I want all the details."

I then went on to tell Sarah (and the rest of the New-Do posse) all about the wonderful day I had with Rachael. The galleries we visited, our trip to the National Seashore, the lunch we shared, and the wonderful hike we took. Once I started talking, it was with teenage enthusiasm, I was a babbling machine. Time flew by at what seemed like 500 knots, the speed of a commercial airliner. Before I knew it, my hair looked great and I was over-tipping Sarah. She gave me a hug, a wink, and said, "Good luck with that girl of yours." Just as you probably suspect, I was given another round of applause on the way out the door.

"Don't worry, Michael, I won't embarrass you next time you're in." Sarah's last words faded into a chorus of laughter as I walked out of the salon. Folks, I honestly loved every minute of my time in New-Do. The laughter was genuine, good-natured, and for a guy who lives alone; very welcoming, playful teasing.

\*

Okay, it's time to get back to my main tale. When I finally made it to the library, Rachael acted as if she had seen me yesterday and not three days ago. She was carefree and enthusiastic about what she called our next "date" to search for the Hartley painting. I know I don't have to tell you, but I am. You can only guess what the word "date" coming from Rachael did to me, Yowzah!

The month of March zipped by, and even though we visited a dozen galleries we made little progress in our search, and before I knew it, Rachael was tied up at work preparing for April school vacation. Our relationship hadn't advanced much since our first venture into Eastham. Don't get me wrong, we had a great time and a ton of laughs. Rachael really loves the outdoors and hiking; she readily shares her experiences with me. On the investigative front, our progress was analogous to a car stuck in Louisiana mud. Most of the art galleries and antique shops we found open, were getting their stores prepared for the tourist season. We managed to speak with several of the owners, artist, and employees, but no one recalled the Hartley Farm painting or anything like what we described.

With Rachael occupied with library business I took the opportunity to stop by and update Kitten on the hunt for the Hartley Farm painting. When I first showed her the letter and my research, she was very excited, and wanted to be kept updated.

True to form, when I walked into Kitten's office she asked, "Sailor Boy, how's your love life with that librarian of yours?"

"Kitten, I'm still in the batter's box, and the count's not in my favor."

"From what I saw the day you and Rachael came to see me about this mystery of yours, you should be rounding second base."

"I'll be happy with getting to first base."

"Well, the real mystery is why you haven't scored!"

Kitten enjoyed seeing me tongue-tied and watching my embarrassment. She roared with laughter and said, "Don't be so shy Michael, that beautiful woman is taken with you. If you don't make your move soon, she may abandon you and you'll be stuck with me."

"If I wasn't an honorable guy, I'd be dating the two of you."

"Now, that's what I want to hear, Sailor Boy."

When we'd stopped laughing, I filled Kitten in on the search. She told me not to get discouraged and said, "If Jane from the Historical Society told you there's a painting, you'll find it. Besides, the more time you spend with Rachael, the better the odds you'll end up hitting a home run and scoring after all."

Kitten got a real kick out of me blushing at her good-natured boldness. But like I told you, Rachael's out of my league. Rest assured though; I may not be fast, smooth, or cool but I'm not giving up.

With school vacation in the past, I was eager to continue our investigation. Rachael and I decided to make one last pass through Eastham and Orleans before we turned our attention to Brewster. We spent a fairly exhausting day in search of the painting without much luck.

Once again, we ended up at the Salt Pond Visitor Center. The late April sun blazed bright and we were rewarded with a mid-afternoon in the low sixty degrees. After eating a light lunch, we decided to walk the Nauset Bicycle Trail. A nearly four-mile round trip walk on a paved surface of rolling and challenging knolls for the casual biker. The smooth, asphalt surface is perfect for the walker. The trail weaves its way through a wonderland of pines and connects with Nauset Beach.

As you near the end of the trail, you come to a wooden walkway that serves as a bridge over the marsh. Water flows underneath the weathered planks. It's a location that offers a picturesque view—a vantage point to stop and admire the wonderful scenery that surrounds you. I was glad I had brought my binoculars with me. We zoomed in on the colorful flowers and the magnificent birds that make the complex wetland their habitat. Rachael has a better knowledge of the birds and flowers we were viewing. She loves to good-naturedly quiz me about what we're seeing. As you know, I'm a rockhead when it comes to remembering the names of birds and flowers, but I'm completely fascinated by the bright, distinct colors.

My mind drifted as I looked up into the cloudless, pale-blue sky. I was in awe watching the soaring seagulls flying overhead. The skill of these birds as they glide transforms them from beach scavengers, to the most majestic of Aves. There's a stateliness to their performance. They gracefully cut through the air displaying their aeronautical prowess. The reverence I feel toward the birds gliding overhead is the same admiration that keeps me returning to the stone pedestal at Quivett Neck. I'm drawn to the hard surface of a century's old rock formation, a prime seat for watching the courageous, lone gull soar in wonderment.

As we continued to admire the view from the wooden promenade, I could feel Rachael staring at me. My sense, she was trying to decide whether or not to ask me something. Instead of continuing to appreciate the artful motion of the birds overhead, I turned my attention toward Rachael, and looked directly at her.

"What's your story, Michael?"

I was surprised by her question. We had avoided personal inquiries since the day Rachael called me Mr. Money. My intention wasn't to avoid talking about my past with her. I just wasn't sure how much to reveal or how soon, so I said, "I guess it's not much of a story…I joined the Navy at eighteen and retired twenty years later. When I was honorably discharged in San Diego, I bought a truck and drove around the country visiting all the places I'd read about over the years. When I got to Cape Cod, I sort of ran out of road."

Rachael's look was penetrating, I could sense she wanted to know more, but didn't push. I reciprocated and asked, "What's your story, Rachael, I'm sure it's much more interesting than mine?"

Laughing, she said, "College at the University of Virginia, where I'd studied library science. I'd always wanted to be a librarian, but things didn't work out the way I'd hoped. I was sidetracked for twelve years and now I'm a librarian and enjoying every moment of it."

Just as I'd been vague, Rachael was equally hazy explaining her past. I hadn't thought she was any more evasive than me. My guess, she was guarding her previous life exactly as I had. We were like two people verbally jousting, trying to feel each other out. Unsure of how much and how soon to share our stories, so we danced around the edges of our past. However, I was sure of one thing, Rachael wanted to know my full story, and I definitely wanted to know all I could about this beautiful, smart, and caring woman with a fruity scent who was standing next to me. We would definitely share our stories when the time was right, of that, I was certain.

The Nauset trail conveniently ended where I'd parked my truck. We then started home to Dennis. On the way, Rachael suggested we stop so she could show me Skaket Beach. While exploring Eastham and Orleans, we had spent the majority of our time in search of the Hartley Farm painting or taking in the beauty of the National Seashore. Rachael told me how much she loved the contrast between the Atlantic surf and the serenity of the bayside beaches. She loves Skaket in Orleans, particularly when the tide recedes and the sun is setting across the bay.

The parking lot was nearly empty when we arrived. We parked close to the sand near an old, wooden lifeguard tower with white, peeling paint. The air had turned quite crisp, and it was getting late in the day for beachgoers. A dark cloud cover was setting in to discourage sunset watchers from migrating to the soft sand of the beach to catch a last glint of light over the bay. As luck would have it, low tide was at its peak, accentuating the clarity of the small white caps as the tiny breakers bubbled up on shore. A shoal had formed as water from the bay created shallow pools.

I grabbed an old blanket from the trunk concealed in the bed of my Ridgeline. We laid the gray, U.S. Navy wool throw on the soft, khaki colored sand and rested our bodies inches from each other. Sitting next to Rachael, I'd like to tell you my heart was beating to the slow rhythm of the waves, but you know that's not true. Only Seabiscuit knows the pounding in my chest as he lumbered to victory over War Admiral.

I longed for the talent to capture nature from the eyes and words of the giants of environmental writing like Thoreau, Emerson, John Burroughs, and Susan Fenimore Cooper. A skill that escapes this humble Navy man with his modest story. Like with birds and flowers, I write with simple words—what my eyes see and my heart feels.

The early evening chill brought Rachael physically closer to me. I could feel the warmth of her body; mine was like a furnace. I distracted my desire to embrace her by concentrating on the natural surroundings. With discernment my mind absorbed the changes the retreating tide left behind. I watched as pools of saltwater formed, and streams of water weaved around seductively-rich, green seagrass. There were patches of withered flora shooting up from the sand. Wheat colored grass flowed gracefully as it was swept by the brush of the soft sea breeze. The gentle wind created wrinkles in the hard sand near the water's edge. A reminder of the dune ripples in the Mojave Desert; a scenic beauty located in my home state of California.

As we continued to sit admiring the serenity of the bay, the thin wafer of a sand dollar was all that separated us. Rachael spoke of our hunt for the painting, suggesting it was time to expand our search pattern. My proximity to her as she talked nearly paralyzed me, but I managed to nod in agreement. At Rachael's suggestion, and my mechanical head bobbing, we concurred it was time to broaden the scope of our search to Brewster. There are plenty of galleries and antique shops for us to investigate in the quaint, bayside community. Rachael said, "Brewster offers so many diverse opportunities to experience nature. There are wonderful local and state parks, majestic hiking trails, and breathtaking beaches for us to explore."

Our reward for lingering on the sand that spring night was a glimpse of the sun dipping through the graying, altostratus clouds. A glowing reflection created by the bright rays bounced off the water. Shades of brilliant red streamed between the menacing cloud cover and the salty bay. Rachael and I remained welded together until the orangey-reddish sphere seemingly penetrated the water.

Stopping at Skaket Beach put an exclamation mark to highlight a perfect day. The ride home left me hopeful and excited about the future. Our search for the mysterious painting would expand to a new town. On the relationship front, Rachael and I would get to spend more time together. Hopefully, my comfort level with her would extend to something more than emotional paralysis. All in all, life was looking good for me on Cape Cod. The weather was improving, summer would be here before you knew it, and my friendship with Rachael was evolving daily.

*

I'd become pretty friendly with Marco and we made plans to go fishing together. He's a regular angler, while I'm more of a novice, but more than willing to learn. Marco spent his youth in the port town of Sant Pol de Mar in the Catalonia region of Spain. Many a day he would go fishing with his grandfather in a small boat called a "barco pequeno." The tiny wooden craft with its chipped paint, two seats, and leaky, round-bottom hull made fishing more of a chore than an adventure.

While Marco loved his time at sea on both large ships and small boats of his youth, he now prefers to fish from shore. He'll sometimes cast-off the jetties on evenings when the advancing tide carries hungry fish into the food-rich marshland, but mostly, he enjoys the thrill of surfcasting as waves rush toward shore.

Marco picked me up at my house and we headed over to Quivett Neck. He told me some people refer to the area as Brewster Flats and for good reason. When the tide is out you can walk for miles over the pancake surface. Marco keeps an old jeep, the perfect jalopy for navigating the rough, dirt road that he uses to traverse the narrow path through shrubs and trees. The price of passage was the tiger-like claw scrapes slashed against the side of his vehicle. Once we arrived near the water's edge, Marco had me exit his jeep so he could wrestle his four-wheeler into a sandy, shrub lined nook.

Since I'm not a regular fisherman, Marco lent me his spare waders and a fishing pole with a Penn reel. I'd fished many times as a kid and on occasion in the Navy, so I wasn't completely inexperienced, only out of practice.

It didn't take me long to get into the groove of surfcasting. Marco used a two-hook bent minnow to start and he set me up with his favorite, a slim, shiny green and yellow, rear-hook jig with dark, penetrating eyes. All of his lures were mounted with de-barbed J or circle hooks.

The water was cold, but I was dry and content in the borrowed rubber waders. Within an hour Marco had hooked two striped bass. Both were keepers above the twenty-eight inch minimum—one was thirty-two and the other thirty-four. I snagged plenty of brownish seaweed before I reeled in a hard-fighting blue. These tough fish have an oily, pungent taste, and are not the best for eating. Freeing the Bluefish to swim another day was a better option. I kept it submerged while I removed the circle hook from its mouth. With regained independence, the silvery, game fish quickly swam away. Marco had given me a tutorial on the proper method of hook removal and safe handling of fish. This practice is commonly known as "catch and release."

By the end of the day, my buddy caught another thirty-four-inch bass, while I snared a thirty-two for my first striper. After cleaning our fish, we put the white meat on ice. Marco insisted we split the day's catch evenly. When I got home, I wrapped the stripers in plastic and placed the tender meat in the freezer for a special occasion. Wink, wink, you know who I would love to grill those babies for!

Once the warmer weather of May arrived, I found myself hanging out at the house with Sailor and grilling more often rather than going out to eat. I really enjoyed the home life, and while I liked the comradery of the local pubs, nothing could compare with the satisfaction of enjoying a good meal, and a cold brew, on my peaceful piece of Cape Cod.

With a certain amount of boldness, I looked at my best buddy and said, "Sailor, it's time for me to invite Rachael over for dinner." I got a couple of barks out of the pooch, he wasn't wagging his tail, so I couldn't tell if he thought it was a good idea or warning me of an impending disaster. Now, all I needed to do was to get up the nerve and invite Rachael over for a nice, home cooked meal—easy, right? Hah!

My plan was to ask Rachael over for dinner under the guise of a strategy meeting to discuss our continuing investigation. Here was my argument for getting together, "Rachael, Brewster's rich in fine art galleries, antique shops, and a host of retail stores offering tasteful replicas and memorabilia of Cape Cod. If we're to be successful in our search, there's no better way than for us to discuss the best approach to moving forward while enjoying a good meal." A simple compilation of words I kept rehearsing to myself in order to gain the confidence needed to invite Rachael to my house for a home cooked meal.

The next morning I went for a hard run and grabbed a shower before heading over to the library. Exercise was a sure way for me to burn off energy, let my body unwind, and build up the courage to nonchalantly approach Rachael with my proposition. I wanted to be at ease when I casually asked Rachael over for dinner. Like that's possible for me when it comes to you-know-who.

On my way over to the library, I stopped at double Ds and discovered, it's now just Ds, no more double Ds. So, I ordered my usual hot, strong, and black coffee. Funny, the brew tasted the same as when it was still double Ds. With a jolt of caffeine courage, I was ready to approach Rachael with my proposal.

When I arrived at the library, Rachael was busy helping a line of patrons checking out books. I found myself a quiet spot to read, drink my coffee, and think about the Hartley Farm. Okay, I'm sure you guessed it, I didn't spend my time reading, drinking my coffee, or reflecting on the Hartley Farm. I used the time waiting for Rachael to rehearse the script I'd prepared to ask her over for dinner. Precisely how long I'd spent practicing for my big moment became evident when I took a sip of my now cold, black coffee.

My partner was pretty busy for a midweek morning. When things slowed down, with cat-like speed, I made my move. I enticed Rachael by telling her about my fishing expedition with Marco, and the haul of strippers we caught. To my surprise, Rachael practically invited herself. When I mumbled something about home cooking, her response was an enthusiastic, "Yes." My heart broke the world high jump record even though the rest of my body never left the floor. All I could remember of our conversation was that I was having company at my place the next night.

Sailor knew Rachael was coming to dinner before I entered the house. His tail was wagging and he was singing a happy bark. My raspy howling of the lyrics to the *Greatest Love Story* by LANCO, I had just heard on the radio, was a dead give-away that this Navy man was one, happy camper.

Exactly as the weather person predicted, the evening of our unofficial date was perfect for eating outdoors. The firepit would provide a romantic glow. My playlist of country music softly serenading us in the background would set a casual mood. With the way I get tongue tied around Rachael, I prayed she would carry the conversation and the evening would be a great success.

Okay, a couple things in case you're wondering. What I know about wooing a woman, I'd read in *O, The*

*Oprah Magazine.* I hadn't actually applied the advice, so don't expect much. And, if I hadn't already mentioned it, the fire pit and grill are tied to my gas line—like I don't sound like a broken record, a little convenience, and no smoky disaster, was what I needed to make the night a hit.

I kept the menu pretty simple, two good size stripers, fresh vegetables, and a garden salad. My seasoning of choice is called *Hidden Core Lemon Garlic.* During my travels I picked it up in a quaint spice shop in Franklin, Tennessee. The savory flavoring is a mild seasoning that can be sprinkled directly onto the food or for marinating. Rachael drinks white wine and I'm usually a beer man who, on occasion, likes a good red wine. Prior to Rachael's arrival I had the table on the patio set by following the simple rules of Emily Post; and the food I'd prepared was keeping cold in the refrigerator.

Rachael arrived at seven with a grand smile, and a fruit salad for dessert. She was wearing a pair of light, tan capris with a peach colored top, and a complementary peach sweater wrapped around her shoulders. When she greeted me, she gave me a kiss on the cheek, and thanked me for having her over for dinner. Rachael's soft lips touching my face sent a bolt of lightning through me. The warm tingle of her kiss lingered as we parted. The sensation lasted long enough for me to take in her beauty. The slight separation gave Sailor an opportunity to muscle his way past me. He was hamming it up and fawning all over Rachael. The lucky stiff was wrapped in her arms licking my girl's face. I was getting close to buying my roomie an express ticket to the dog pound!

The rude intrusion of my mate gave me time to recover from Rachael's kiss and regain my composure. With Sailor attached to Rachael's side, I gave her the grand tour of my small but comfortable abode. Rachael loved the house and commented on how tastefully it looked. Most of the artwork I'd purchased came from art and craft fairs. These venues gave local artists the opportunity to showcase their unique creations. I hadn't spared any expense on the furniture. The truth be told, I'm really not an astute or creative shopper. My strategy was to buy the whole ensemble on display and leave the creativity to the professionals. Rachael was pleasantly surprised my humble home wasn't the typical single guys, man cave.

After the tour, we made small talk as I poured her a glass of wine and grabbed a Bud for myself. We, now a trio with the inclusion of the four-legged intruder, made our way outdoors and sat at the patio table enjoying our drinks. I lit the grill and waited for it to heat up. When the temperature was right, I laid the fish and vegetables over the cast-iron grates. The smell of the chow aroused my hunger and attracted Rachael's attention. She said, "The food smells delicious Michael, another pleasant surprise from the mysterious Navy man."

I didn't verbally comment to her, instead, responded with a broad smile that concealed my nervousness. I didn't want Rachael to be disappointed with my cooking; insecurity had me doubting my culinary skills. All I kept thinking was, I hope it tastes as good as it smells.

When the food was ready, we sat across from each other eating our meal. Sailor coyly nestled against Rachael's feet and remained on his best behavior. Our conversation was casual and Rachael was full of compliments, repeatedly praising my skills as a grill master. She couldn't help ribbing me when she said, "The striper was delicious, I must have eaten the one Marco caught." I couldn't argue with her; she was probably right.

Once we finished our meal, Rachael helped me clean the table and load the dishwasher while the little chowhound sniffed around for scraps.

I grabbed myself a second beer while Rachael deferred. Her glass was still half-full. The fire pit was glowing and we were sitting comfortably on Adirondack chairs with thick, floral patterned seat cushions. Sailor rested his warm body between us. He looked at me with his big brown eyes to let me know, he was the mate and I was still the skipper. It didn't take long before the pretentious pup was brushing up against Rachael. So much for the chain of command, it was now man versus dog for the librarian's heart.

"Thank you for inviting me over for dinner, it was wonderful."

"Thank you for accepting, I was nervous asking you, but thrilled you accepted."

"I'm not sure why you'd be nervous, we've spent a lot of time together between the library and on the search for the Hartley painting."

"I guess after twenty years in the Navy and never staying in one place for too long, you spend most of your time with acquittances and not with real friends."

"Well, thank you for thinking of me as your friend, it's very thoughtful of you. It looks like you firmly planted roots on Cape Cod and I'm glad you did."

"I never officially apologized for buying you Christmas presents, I didn't mean for you to be uncomfortable or for you to reciprocate."

"At the time, I was taken by surprise by the amount of money you must have spent, and I was uneasy with accepting the gifts."

"It wasn't my intention. I know how much you enjoyed *Dangerous Ambition* and admire Dorothy Thompson. When I saw the signed copy of her political guide and Hertog's book on the Internet, I bought them."

"I very much appreciate the gifts; it was generous of you. I've always found Dorothy Thompson to be an exceptional woman. After reading *Dangerous Ambitions,* I gained a real perspective of the struggle she had balancing her love life with an amazing, high-level career.

"Think of how hard women had to fight for the right to vote. It wasn't until 1920 that the nineteenth amendment was ratified and women could finally cast their ballot. And...within twenty years, you have this strong, smart woman with tremendous influence expressing her views as a columnist in major newspapers. This was all during a critical period in our history. While I don't always agree with Dorothy Thompson's politics, what fascinates me is she was one of the most influential journalists and commentators in the country. She had enormous influence with Franklin and Eleanor Roosevelt and the events leading up to America's involvement in World War II."

"I can hear it in your voice how passionate you are about her."

"It's not only her, I'm fascinated by women who became powerful professionally during the mid-twentieth century. My three favorite women are Dorothy Thompson, Eleanor Roosevelt, and Martha Gellhorn. Eleanor wasn't simply a first lady; she wrote a newspaper column that was read by millions of people and Martha was a writer and war correspondent. She covered every war from the Spanish Civil War in the late 1930s, World War II, Vietnam, and the U.S. invasion of Panama in 1989."

"You sound more like a historian than a librarian."

"I think we should all be historians of a sort, remembering the past helps to understand the present and the future. We should celebrate the good and learn from the bad. There's no denying that our historical legacy is fraught with blemishes. It wasn't until the early 1970s, a mere fifty years ago, that many traditional male colleges and universities finally opened their doors to women. A lot has changed in the last one hundred years since women earned their right to vote, and much more still needs to change. Reading and taking the time to understand this historical evolution makes you better informed. That's why I love being a librarian, you're exposed to so many books and ideas on such interesting and diverse topics. It makes it easy to stay informed and remember the past."

"Why did you become an analyst for the FBI when you have such a passion for being a librarian?"

"I think your question is for another day. It's getting late and I have to work in the morning. Thank you again for such a wonderful time."

"And, thank you for the history lesson. We tend to take so much for granted today, not realizing the changes that have taken place in a short period of time. But still, I find it shocking to think it has been only one hundred years since women earned the right to vote in our country. It's so true, those pioneering women who championed the right to vote and who challenged the status quo should always be remembered."

"You're a good student, Sailor Man."

Rachael gave me another kiss on the cheek while the pup got a heck of a lot more love than me. My remorseful buddy, looking to regain my affection, cozied up to me as we stood in the driveway waving goodbye to Rachael. We waited until her car faded into the darkness before heading inside. It was a wonderful evening despite my meddlesome four-legged friend. I was gaining new insight into Rachael every time we were together. I felt confident if we were going to have a future there was much more we needed to willingly tell each other.

After our dinner date I took a day off from the library, and spent the day working around the house. Low tide near Sesuit Harbor had rolled back by five in the afternoon. I took the little critter, who literally worked his way out of the doghouse by unabashedly sucking up to me, for a walk on the beach. It was good exercise for him to frolic and run on the hard, sandy surface. My first mate adapted to the water as naturally as a Navy Seal. He would attack the small waves as they broke near the shore like a linebacker charging the quarterback. When the wet, sandy pooch had enough of the saltwater, we headed home. The outside shower made bathing him easy. Like me, Sailor wasn't interested in a two-minute shower. He was as playful under the misty spray, as a toddler enjoying a bath with a tub full of toys. All of this activity tired him out, and it wasn't long before he was curled up on the couch fast asleep.

Once the tired-out tyke was softly snoring, I headed over to the Mad Dawg Pub. When I got there it hadn't taken long for me to realize my heart wasn't into it. All I had thought about was seeing Rachael again. I couldn't wait to return to the library and spend time with her. Our next date to search for the Hartley Farm painting seemed so far away, like crossing the Mediterranean Sea in a rowboat. After one beer, this love-struck sailor headed home, and I was glad I did. The last rays of daylight were merging with the evening darkness. There was just enough light to cast a fading shadow as my little buddy and I took a short walk before nestling into a cozy night.

As luck would have it, Rachael called my cell phone shortly after I arrived back at the house. Sailor knew instinctively who it was and gave a cheerful bark. Rachael told me she'd switched her day off to help out a coworker and wondered if I was available to continue our search in the morning. I'm not sure I concealed my enthusiasm. My guess, she didn't need to hear me say yes to know I was thrilled to pick her up the next day.

Rachael was waiting outside of her house when I arrived. She was dressed in hiking shoes, tan slacks, a white V-neck tee shirt, and a jean jacket. She was toting a backpack and a small collapsible cooler containing our lunch. Her face held a healthy tan, and with her sporty, Ray-Ban sunglasses and dark, wavy hair she looked awfully sexy.

We spent the morning visiting shops in Brewster without much luck. Around noon, we stopped at Avellino's Antiques and Artistry to have a look around. As we entered the shop, it didn't look like the type of gallery that would carry a painting such as the Hartley Farm. The theme was more natural landscapes, animals, and habitats of the Cape. There were spectacular scenes of the Outer-Cape. The artistry brought the dunes of Provincetown to life by artfully integrating the indigenous creatures and native vegetation into the rugged terrain.

Rachael headed toward the rear of the shop while I moseyed through the aisles. My eyes focused on the artwork, antique statues, and sculptures on exhibit. The intrusion of a seagull's screech rang in my head, drawing my attention to a seemingly modest painting of a lone, white gull rising toward a setting sun. I held my gaze; my eyes were locked on the artist's creation of a beautiful seagull. Suddenly, as if by magic, the seabird transformed into an enchanting dove.

While I stood as still as the Washington Monument, mesmerized by the artistic illusion, Rachael was approached by a tall, slim male who introduced himself as Andrew. Like two old friends, they were engaged in an amiable conversation.

After a few minutes of talking with Andrew, Rachael called over to me breaking my hypnotic concentration. I couldn't help but smile at the wizardry of the artist when, as if by hocus-pocus, the painted seagull mysteriously reappeared. I headed over to Rachael, who made the introductions. Andrew then continued talking and said, "I certainly remember the Rose Gallery. Rose was such a wonderful woman; her studio was filled with beautiful artwork. She also had a penchant for laying out beautiful bouquets of roses. It was always the same four colors red, white, pink, and yellow.

"As I was about to tell Rachael, I know the Hartley painting well; it was an expensive rendition of a mid-eighteen hundreds farm. Rose would talk of the painting as if the artistry had a story to tell but she couldn't understand what it had to say. It was clearly her favorite, she always had an excuse not to sell it. There had been some very good offers to purchase it, but Rose would say the buyer wasn't right and she would only sell to the special person who could hear what the painting had to say."

Rachael asked, "Do you know if she sold it to another gallery when she closed her shop?"

"I can't say for sure, but I recall Rose saying all the buyers who purchased her inventory were from galleries along 6A. If she sold the Hartley painting when she liquidated, you'll probably find it along that road. My shop's not in the same market as Rose's, and to her disappointment, I wasn't able to hear what the painting had to say. Every time I entered her shop she would say, 'Andrew, listen closely, are you sure you can't hear what the painting is saying.'" I hated to admit I couldn't…She was such a loveable woman; I greatly enjoyed the time I'd spent in her gallery admiring the artwork she showcased."

We thanked Andrew for the information, I then asked him to explain the painting of the lone seagull. Andrew became slightly animated as he said, "That's my mom's favorite, she's the artist and calls it *Margaret's Dove*. For her, the painting represents hope, peace, and love."

"I was completely transfixed by the painting. My mind played tricks on me, as I stared at the seagull, suddenly I imagined a dove."

"Your mind didn't deceive you. My mom created a symmetry between her two favorite birds with a phantasm not many people can see. You have a fine eye for seeing the artist's interpretation."

Rachael interjected with a smile and said, "Michael is full of surprises and his artistic talent looks to be no exception." Pausing, she winked at me and said, "I think with a little persuasion, he may purchase your mother's favorite painting…I would love to see it."

"I may be full of surprises, but Rachael's the artist."

"Really, I would love to see your work, I'm always looking for new talent."

"Michael's exaggerating, I'm only an amateur who likes to sketch natural scenes of Cape Cod."

"Still, I would be happy to see your work."

"Thank you, I certainly will think about it."

"Please do, and don't be inhibited. I find artists to be their own harshest critic."

The three of us walked over to the aisle where *Margaret's Dove* was showcased. Again, I concentrated on the seagull, and was taken aback by the apparition of a dove. Rachael said, "How beautiful, what a detailed likeness to an all-white seagull. It looks as if it could fly off the canvas. Your mother created an interesting perspective of the gull. Looking at the painting, I see a bird in flight, suddenly motionless, yet suspended in the air."

"That's an accurate observation. My mom wanted to show the majesty she sees in the seagull. She didn't want to paint a static bird, she wanted to show how dynamic and graceful they are."

"Your mother is quite an accomplished artist," said Rachael

"Thank you, I would love for you to meet her, but she's working in her studio and I usually don't disturb her."

The dove never materialized for Rachael. She later told me she truly loved the painting but wished she could've seen what I'd seen. Without much prodding from Andrew, I purchased the painting signed by his mother, Meg Avellino. Neither Rachael nor I blinked when we were told the price. She merely smiled in wonder as I wrote a five-figure check. Before the ink was dry, an attractive woman, mid-sixties, dark hair cut short, stylishly elegant, wearing a soothing, lavender, crepe sheath dress introduced herself as Meg Avellino.

"Thank you for purchasing the painting. I was working in my studio when I felt a strong sensation *Margaret's Dove* was about to fly away. I wanted to personally meet and thank the buyer."

"You're very welcome, it's beautiful. I could feel such a strong connection to the painting and immediately knew I had to buy it."

"I'm sure Andrew told you it's my favorite painting. For me, it represents hope, peace, and love." Meg paused for a few moments and said, "I always feel a temporary sadness when I sell one of my paintings, yet I'm happy when a buyer sees value in my work. The seagull has a special meaning to me, I'm thrilled to let one go to a buyer who eyes it with the same majesty as I do. You are a couple truly in love, and I know you will cherish the painting." Meg had stopped speaking, but as if through telepathy, I could her words continuing, "If you believe, and I know you do Michael, the seagull may not always be visible but will guide and protect you on your quest."

I wanted to respond to Meg Avellino but I was at a loss for what to say. Not to mention the reaction I would get from Rachael and Andrew when I told them that I heard Meg's voice in my head.

While I love the painting I'd just bought, more meaningful was Meg's comment that the painting represents hope, peace, and love. The three things needed to capture Rachael's heart and give Mary Hartley a Christian burial. I'm still stunned by Meg's telepathic words," If you believe, and I know you do Michael, the seagull may not always be visible but will guide and protect you on your quest." I had so many questions to ask, but Meg was gone before I could recover from her comments.

Walking out of Avellino's Antiques and Artistry, it felt really good to have another confirmation that a rendition of a mid-eighteen hundreds farm had been on display at the Rose Gallery. Even though the information brought us no closer to finding the painting; hearing that an expensive portrait of a farm with the transcendental qualities Rose sold, energized me. Meg's parting words suggested she knew my connection and admiration for seagulls. The mysticism of her psychic communication left me with a warm, comforting feeling.

Rachael was upbeat when she said, "I know in my heart we're on the right path; it may take time, but I believe we'll find the Hartley Farm painting and give Mary Hartley a proper, Christian burial. Meg Avellino is a wonderful woman, her comments were otherworldly. I'm beginning to believe there's more to our search than even we realize."

Rachael's words had my mind wrapped in what seemed like a charged up Ford zooming around the racetrack at the Daytona 500. The Hartley mystery was cloaked in so many supernatural manifestations. There were my dreams of Mary Hartley, her voice speaking to me, the elusive and mysterious painting, and now Meg's cryptic comments of a fabled seagull. I pushed aside these thoughts and tried to focus on the facts. The truth was we weren't much closer to finding the Hartley painting than when we started. Maybe a little belief in the ghostly world would turn out to be a good thing.

By mid-afternoon, we were having lunch at Nickerson State Park. With over nineteen hundred acres of land, there was plenty to do at this public, recreation paradise. There are trails that weave their way through dense woods and around scenic ponds. One can let their imagination wander to the days of the early pioneers exploring the pristine wilderness of the Cape. You can almost feel the ghostly presence of the Nauset and other Native American tribes who were forced from the land of their birth.

Rachael and I looked over the park map and decided to hike the nearly three-mile trail around Cliff Pond. We walked along a narrow path laden with brownish pine needles. The trail was wedged between trees, shrubs, and the lake. The sound, sights, and smells of the forest accompanied us on our journey. Like a magnet, we were pulled toward sandy nooks offering a view of the sun's glimmer as it reflected off the pond. The weather was warm, the water tabletop calm, and so inviting. As we were nearing the end of our hike we stood in a small opening between two trees. Across the pond, the stage light focus of the sun bounced off the trees lining the bank creating a mirror's reflection in the water. It was as if a magic looking glass captured the personality and beauty of the trees, not for us humble spectators, but for the trees themselves.

On the way home, my thoughts drifted between Rachael, Nickerson Park, and Meg's words, "You are a couple truly in love." I wondered, what did she see when Rachael and I were standing side by side? Was there an aura we shared that said, "You are in love!" Unlike me, who's heart could have been cited for speeding by the police, Rachael let the words pass without comment and hadn't seemed fazed by them. I wasn't going to raise the subject; I'd leave it up to Rachael.

We made one final stop for a little nourishment at the Brewster Mercantile. The building was built in the 1850s and converted into a general store in the 1860s. Upon entering the shop we immediately noticed the exquisite craftsmanship of the antique counters and shelves. The well-maintained, glossy, mahogany interior made me feel like a time traveler entering a bygone century. The store sells a wide assortment of goods, snacks, and old fashioned, penny candy. Rachael ordered a cold drink and a small piece of fudge and I opted for a coffee.

We sat in front of the store on one of the weather worn, wooden benches enjoying our refreshments and talking. I was slowly becoming comfortable with Rachael and had shed some of my inhibitions. My transformation was owed more to Rachael's personality and graciousness than any great awakening on my part. It had almost felt natural when I asked, "I was wondering if you're free over the weekend?"

"I'm working Saturday until four and have plans for Sunday. What did you have in mind?"

"I thought maybe we could take Sailor down to the beach when you get out of work on Saturday. Afterword, I can cook dinner for us."

"It sounds like you're asking me on a date?"

I was initially tongue tied, but recovered and said, "Let's call it a pre-date, if it was a real date, I would take you to a very nice and pricey restaurant."

"Well Sailor Boy, I'm going to consider this a date. As for a nice and pricey meal, I'll take a walk on the beach and home cooking any day."

"A date it is," was my lame response.

Here's the thing, I keep playing this conversation over in my head and keep coming up with the most optimistic conclusion. Rachael, the woman of my dreams, accepted a date with me. Wow! Wow! And Wow!

Saturday couldn't get here fast enough. The forecaster's prediction called for sunshine and a light breeze, perfect weather for a late afternoon walk on the beach and barbecuing. When Rachael arrived at my place, she gave me a warm, squeezing hug and a kiss on the cheek. As we held the embrace, I lavished in her fragrance. Her scent was clean and fresh with a fruity fragrance of apples and pomegranate. She was dressed in jeans, a sleeveless, yellow top, and sandals. My date, I love the sound of those two words, looked and smelled hotter than the inferno building inside of me. Too late for me to take a cold shower! It would be like throwing water on rocks in a sauna.

Unlike me, Sailor had no inhibition. He was excited to see Rachael again; his tail was wagging and he was bouncing around hamming it up. Rachael loved it, and of course, I was as jealous as a kid without an ice cream. To make matters worse, she gave the wide-eyed pup a longer hug and kiss. It seemed like forever until the two finally separated. Once apart, we headed over to Cold Storage Beach. The parking lot was a quarter full when we arrived. Rachael removed her sandals and I took off my boat shoes. We left them on an ocean-blue, pressure-treated plank with the words "Shoe Parking," painted across the board.

When I let Sailor off of his leash, he dashed right for the salty water. We then shot after him like a couple of greyhounds chasing a mechanical lure. We were no match for the four-legged speedster as he beat us to the water. True to form, my Academy Award winning mate put on one big, grand performance. He raced around with me and Rachael in pursuit. You guessed it, he always let Rachael catch him, so he could get a big hug. Her reward from the furry pup was wet and sandy clothes that she good-naturedly brushed off. I had brought a floating, retrievable toy and had Sailor charging after it, plunging fearlessly into the surf. My throws into the bay went further with every toss and Sailor reveled in the challenge.

After the pooch shook off the saltwater, we took a short walk along the shore and when Sailor was sufficiently dried, we returned to my truck. Rachael insisted on toweling off the big-headed showboat as he basked in her attention. Dried and content, my little mate hopped into the rear passenger area. When we arrived at my house, the wiped-out little tyke made his way to his bed, and was soon in a deep slumber, spread out on the soft, faux fur.

With the pouch catching some Z's, I finally had Rachael to myself. Once the grill was lit and the food cooking, we sat lounging around the fire pit. Rachael had a white wine and I had a glass of red wine. As we talked, Rachael gave me a rundown on her day at the library. I loved listening quietly as she talked of work, expressing the joy of being surrounded by books and the people who love them. As she shared the details of her day, I could feel she was connecting me to a very important part of her life.

During dinner, I spoke about the renovations I'd made to the house, my friend Marco, and the local haunts where I regularly grabbed a bite to eat. Mostly, we kept the conversation light and casual.

With the cleanup completed, we watched the sun setting out over the horizon. The gas fire pit was burning bright, and a quiet between us set in. Our eyes fixed on the glow of the sparkling bluish-red flame. I was the first to speak and asked, "So, what brought you to the Cape?"

Rachael hesitated for a moment, then said, "When I was a little girl, through my teenage years, my family vacationed on Cape Cod. Every summer, we would spend two weeks in a rented cottage, and I have wonderful memories of those years. Moving to this delightful place gives me a sense of comfort knowing how much my family enjoyed vacationing here."

"Leaving the FBI must have been a difficult decision?"

Rachael gave out a nervous laugh and said, "Not really, I enjoyed my time working as an analyst, but my heart was never in it."

"How did you become an analyst when you wanted to be a librarian?"

"I guess when you're young and in love you don't always make the best decisions. How about you, you went into the Navy at eighteen, do you have any regrets?"

"No, I've never regretted joining the Navy or my twenty-year career. That was my goal when I joined. I wanted to retire from the service while I was still young enough to start another chapter in my life. I'm not sure if it's much different from your decision to give up your position as an analyst and start a second career, particularly when you're so passionate about the library."

"How about you, what's your passion?"

"I'm still trying to figure it out. I greatly enjoyed remodeling the house, and the work we've done together searching for the Hartley painting. Both projects have kept me pretty busy. While I was in the Navy, I earned my bachelor's degree in history, so I thought, maybe I'd get my teacher certification and teach high school. Right now, I'm enjoying the freedom of being retired and working with you."

Rachael was silent for a few minutes before she said, "I got married right after graduating from college. I wasn't sure if I was ready for marriage but my future husband was very persuasive. He'd been accepted to law school in Washington DC and wanted us to go there together. It seemed exciting at the time, so I acquiesced and we were married.

"He had attended a job fair right before graduation and without telling me, submitted my resume for a paid summer internship. When I was called by the FBI regarding an analyst position, I was very much surprised. My husband, actually my fiancée at the time, was excited when I told him I'd been contacted by the FBI. He thought it would be great for us to both go to DC and have a job waiting. He had plenty of summer job offers and was narrowing them down before deciding.

"Again, he was very persuasive in his reasoning. He made the case for taking the analyst job for the summer, then in the fall, I could look for a position as a librarian. It came across as logical to me. We could save money over the summer, and if it took time to find a position in a library, we could use our savings until I found employment.

"Well, at the end of the summer, the FBI offered me a full-time position for good money. My husband thought it was great, saying I could keep the job while waiting to hear from one of the many libraries I had applied to. When I finally received a job offer from a local library, the salary was nearly half of what I was making. We wouldn't have been able to pay the bills if I took the library position. Almost daily, he would pressure me with guilt. So, I gave in and stayed with the FBI. Regrettably, I decided to postpone my career as a librarian until my husband graduated from law school."

"Did you look for a librarian position when he graduated?"

Rachael remained quiet for a few minutes as she sat with a far off look in her eyes. When she did respond she said, "For my husband it became a money thing. He was hired by a prestigious firm right out of law school. He wanted to buy a house right away in an affluent neighborhood. So, a reduced income from me didn't fit into his plans. By this time, he was a pro at making me feel guilty when he didn't get his way."

I wasn't sure how to respond to Rachael's story. I had an immediate dislike for her ex-husband, but I didn't want to say something inappropriate. After thinking about it, I said, "You gave up your dream?"

"I did at the time. We were very busy during those years, not only with work but with entertaining. That became a big part of my husbands' plan to advance in the firm or land a position with a top lobbying group. He would spend more and more time away from the house. Then without much notice, he would invite colleagues, clients, or anyone else who could advance his career to our home on the weekends. There was more and more pressure on me to meet his needs and career, while at the same time I had to balance the demands of my job."

As I sat listening to Rachael, it dawned on me to let her talk and not ask any more questions. My sense was

Rachael wanted me to know her story, and at the same time it was a form of catharsis for her.

Rachael continued and said, "After twelve years of marriage, he came home one night and told me he wanted a divorce. Just like that, it was completely out of nowhere. What I later learned; he was having an affair with a lobbyist. She was the person who helped him land a position with a prestigious firm."

"I'm so sorry you had to experience such wretched behavior. It must have been very hard on you."

"The funny thing, when he told me, I started to laugh. It was an honest laugh…I felt such relief. In retrospect, for a few years, our marriage became one of convenience. The hectic pace we'd kept never allowed time to really think about our relationship. As he stood in front of me, I saw him for what he'd always been, a selfish, ambitious, little boy.

"The next day, I gave my notice to the FBI and sent out resumes throughout Cape Cod. With my last paycheck in hand, I packed up my car and headed to Dennis. Job or no job, my mind was made up, Cape Cod would be my new home. As luck would have it, there was a job opening in my new hometown, so I set up an interview. Within a couples of weeks, I was hired and my dream of being a librarian was finally fulfilled."

"Was the divorce contentious?"

"No, on the contrary, our divorce was quick and the settlement generous. I think he was simply relieved there wouldn't be a lot of drama in the breakup of our marriage. He didn't want anything that would sully his professional reputation, so everything went smoothly."

"Well, I'm glad you ended up on the Cape and had the opportunity to work in a position you're passionate about."

"I am too, and I'm glad you also ended up on the Cape. I've loved it here since childhood, and I have such wonderful memories I keep in my heart. There must be more to your story then you sought of ran out of road when you got to Cape Cod?"

"In the Navy, I spent many days and nights out at sea in the worst sorts of weather. While we're all professionals and know our jobs, still, being on deck during a roaring storm is a scary experience. But, it's also stimulating, you experience a survival sensation that shouts out you're alive! It's what happened to me one night when I'd first arrived in Dennis.

"I was awoken on a cold, stormy night by wind that sounded like a roaring locomotive. Rain was pelting off the windows, thunder exploded in sync with the bright flash of lightning. It felt like being under siege and a call for all hands-on deck. I'm not sure what made me do it, but before I knew it, I was dressed in my foul-weather gear and drove down to West Dennis Beach. As the storm raged, I made my way out to the end of the wet, slick jetty and gazed out over the horizon. The sights and sounds of the storm were like a ferocious battle. Everything I was experiencing gave me the feeling of being back at sea. The waves crashing over the stone deck of the jetty, wind gushing against my body as if I was a sail filled with air and a boat heeling over the water, and the rain, a barrage of hailstone pellets ricocheting off my Gore-Tex rain suit.

"When I arrived back at the cottage, I slept the sleep of the dead, and when I awoke, I immediately knew the road I would take and the new home I had found."

"You're a romantic Michael. A storm like the one you experienced when I'd first arrived at the Cape may have sent me packing."

"I can't help feeling there's a link between the storm that kept me on Cape Cod and the Saxby Gale. I feel as if Mary Hartley was testing me before she connected me to her letter. It's the reason I have a strong belief that we will find the painting and discover her remains."

"I too am confident we'll find the painting and arrange for the Christian burial she so desired."

It was getting late, and as much as I didn't want the evening to end, Rachael said she had early plans in the morning. I thanked her for sharing her story with me, and as she was leaving, she kissed me tenderly on the cheek and said, "The next time we get together, it's your turn for show and tell. There's more to your story, Michael Maine, and I can't wait to hear every detail."

As Rachael drove away, my thoughts were on how freely she'd opened up to me, telling me of her marriage. Confiding in me was a big step in our budding relationship. The more time I spent with Rachael, the better I understood her courage and strength. All in all, it was a fantastic day and a perfect ending to the month of May.

*

June arrived the next day and the weather didn't disappoint. I awoke on the first of the month just as the sun began to rise over Nantucket Sound. When I stepped out of my front door, I could feel the warm, bright, rays on my face. As the soothing beam warmed my body, I thought of the poem by Mary Oliver, *"Why I Wake Early."* It's a beautiful poem and my favorite. I love the universal theme of the poetry, and reciting the lyrics is a great way to start your day. You simply welcome the sun warming your face and you begin your day feeling happy and kind. Those beautiful and inspiring words remind me of Rachael. She's always happy, kind, and as bright as the sun. I can't wait to share Mary Oliver's poetry with her.

Recalling the poem, *"Why I Wake Early,"* opened up my senses to the sounds and smells of late spring. Standing in my yard, listening to the tranquil tune of birds, and taking in the fragrance of flowers, made everything about my world more hopeful. Rachael was becoming a big part of my life and I was getting cautiously optimistic about a future together. I had to smile to myself when I thought of June, derived from Juno, the goddess of love and marriage. On this bright sunny morning, I was glad I woke up early.

Rachael had time off midweek, so we made arrangements to visit more galleries in Brewster. Our plan was to search The Gallery by the Bay, The Antique House, and Roisin's Fine Art Gallery. We spent all morning browsing and combing through the three shops, as well as admiring the unique artwork on exhibit. At our third stop, we entered Roisin's gallery. As we walked into the nostalgic looking showroom, we both turned toward each other with wide eyes and broad smiles. Visibly on display were a number of paintings depicting country settings, farms, barns, and farmhouses. A strong fragrance of flowers filled the shop. There were several vases blooming with a combination of red, white, pink, and yellow roses placed throughout the gallery.

We immediately walked over to the area designated, Cape Cod 1800s. As we were looking through racks of posters, prints, and framed paintings, a distinguished looking elderly woman approached us. Her resemblance to the portrait of Rose Flynn was startling. Before I could comment, she said with an Irish brogue, "Good afternoon, I'm Roisin, are you looking for something special or just browsing?"

Rachael and I both responded and said, "Good afternoon."

"Are you interested in 1800s rural settings or farms in general?" asked Roisin.

"Actually, we're looking for a specific painting from the 1860s. It's a rendition of the Hartley Farm," responded Rachael.

"I know the painting you're looking for; it was in the Rose Gallery before it closed. I'm told it's a beautiful representation of the old farm. The artistry is exquisite, but there's an intriguing, allure drawing you to the painting. Hard to articulate, clearly the artist had created a special piece of craftsmanship. It was as if the artwork came to life and had something to tell you. A strong force held your gaze, sizing you up, deciding whether to speak to you. I would often drive to Eastham, simply to admire the depiction of the farm and try to interpret what the image was saying.

"I would talk with Rose about the painting and she felt the same way. She told me she would sit very quietly in front of the Hartley Farm painting and wait for inspiration. Rose was convinced the painting had a story to tell, but she couldn't hear what it was saying.

"As I recall, it was very expensive, and I remember talking with Rose about the cost. She said there had been many good offers but refused to lower the price. In fact, Rose had even thought about increasing the price solely to ensure it wouldn't sell. She was certain the right buyer would one day come along. It's funny, she always insisted she was only the guardian of the painting, like an ancient protector of the Holy Grail. Rose firmly believed there was a special person, honor bound, who would value it, hear what it had to say, and understand what to do. I know it all sounds quite romantic, but the painting did have that effect on you."

"It sounds like a wonderful painting and we would love to see it. Do you happen to know if it was purchased by another gallery?" asked Rachael.

"I recall before Rose passed on; she was able to liquidate her inventory. My memory is another gallery has the painting."

I responded and said, "We've been searching for the painting for months. We visited all the galleries in Eastham, Orleans, and we're working our way through Brewster. Our thoughts are that the Hartley Farm was in Dennis, and the painting would probably remain in one of the neighboring towns."

"I think you're right; I've traveled the Outer Cape visiting most of the galleries and there aren't shops like mine selling landscapes from the 1800s."

Did you ever consider purchasing the Hartley Farm painting?" asked Rachael.

"You know, it wasn't meant to be. When I last drove out to Rose's shop it was shuttered and completely vacated. I made inquiries in the nearby stores and houses. Unfortunately, they all gave conflicting accounts about Rose. Some said she went to stay with family, others mentioned assisted living. However, there was a consensus among the people that I spoke with, the gallery had closed abruptly and they'd heard Rose was very sick. Most of the people didn't think she had much time to live."

"Rose must have been a lovely, special person," said Rachael.

With tears in her eyes, Roisin said, "She certainly was…we had such a spiritual and physical connection; most people thought we were twins. I miss her very much, and the long talks we use to have."

After Roisin regained her composure, I asked, "Would you happen to know Mrs. Murphy or Rose Flynn from Dennis?"

"There's a distant connection, why do you ask?"

"I've seen the portrait of Rose hanging over the mantel in Mrs. Murphy's home and I find your resemblance striking."

"Many of us on Cape Cod came from the coastal town of Kinsale in Ireland. That may explain the resemblance."

I would've liked to have asked Roisin more questions, but I didn't want to come across as rude. There didn't appear to be any other connection to our search except the likeness I saw in her and Rose Flynn. Yet, I felt unsettled in the presence of Roisin; maybe subconsciously it was her admitted likeness to her dear friend Rose from the Rose Gallery.

We extended our appreciation and thanked Roisin for her help. As we were preparing to leave, she gave me her business card, and asked that we call her to let her know if we find the painting.

Rachael and I remained silent as we drove away from Roisin's gallery. I was lost in my own thoughts, trying to separate reality from myth. The truth was, I preferred the saga of a legend than real life. It was romantic to imagine; Rose, the guardian of a painting with magical qualities. Rachael and I, ordained Knights of King Arthur, in search of the Holy Grail.

I was immediately brought back to reality when Rachael directed me to the Stony Brook Grist Mill and Museum. Upon arrival, we strolled the footpaths and wooden walkways lining the enchanting rills. There's a constant flow of water descending over stones hundreds of years old. During late spring the herring travel these brooks on their way to summer spawning pools. Then in autumn, they traverse these same waterways when they return to the cold water of the Atlantic Ocean.

There's a museum housed in an old, wooden building with dark, cedar shakes, and windows trimmed in white to match the antique doors. The historical structure stands as a fortress surrounded by stone walls, greenery, and colorful flowers. An eight-spoke, wooden waterwheel attached to the rock foundation churns with the same rhythm as it did in the 1800s.

The mill provided us with a peaceful and pleasant place to linger and enjoy the enchanting setting. I couldn't help but wonder if Mary Hartley had ever walked these same footpaths.

We could hear the constant, tranquil sound of water moving through the landscape. A flat granite stone provided temporary relief for two tired investigators. We sat overlooking a riffle with swift moving water as it cascaded over weathered rocks creating a miniature Niagara Falls. The constant rush of the runlet fed a pool of clear, calm water. My imagination drifted to a different time when my reflection was captured in the still water of a bathtub sized fountain. Sitting next to me was a sensual woman wearing an open-form bonnet exposing reddish hair and rosy cheeks. When I blinked away the mirage, the beautiful face reflecting off of the water was Rachael.

We continued to take advantage of the bench like qualities of the stone pedestal to sit and watch the water dissipate into the crystal clear pool. The simple joy of sitting next to Rachael stimulated my emotions. Our silence sent my thoughts back to the conversation we had with Roisin. Before I had time to work through her comments, Rachael said, "I've been thinking about the interesting and curious things Roisin had told us. My analytical training compels me to focus on the facts, but I can't help being distracted by the metaphysical aspects weaving through our search.

"There are a number of nagging points that stick with me. We've heard Andrew and Roisin say there's a perception the painting wants to speak and has a story to tell...And, to some extent, seems to control you. Both confirmed Rose felt the same way as they did. Neither Andrew, Roisin, or Rose could understand the message or interpret the artist's perspective. There's an agreement between the three, a buyer does exist, who will hear and understand the painting's message. Roisin told us that Rose felt like she was the ancient protector of the Holy Grail. Her abrupt departure and the closing of her gallery; and, leaving no forwarding information is odd. Finally, and most curious is the three Roses—Rose from the gallery, Rose Flynn, and Roisin, the Irish version of Rose, meaning Little Rose. And, the physical similarity the three shared.

"While I'm intrigued by all this information, my training taught me to characterize these details as questionable. Based strictly on the facts, finding the painting now seems much more elusive. Despite a bias to my training, I'm inclined to accept the more hopeful transcendental nature of this mystery and let my romantic instincts believe we will find the painting."

"When I was first told of the ghost of Old Man Hartley, I completely discounted it. Now I'm obsessed with the apparition of Mary Hartley. These mythical tales of the painting are now a compulsion with me. In fact, I've already fantasized, we're ordained Knights of King Arthur in search of the Holy Grail."

"Well lover boy, don't let those ardent, storybook fantasies of yours consume your thoughts."

I treasured Rachael referring to me as lover boy and couldn't help the Las Vegas size, neon sign plastered across my smiling face. I muttered an unwitty response; I really don't recall what I babbled given my mind froze and my face locked in a scary caricature of a certain president's toothy beam. You know, my nose would look like Pinocchio's if I told you my response to Rachael's comment was witty, cool, and I'd actually remembered it.

After departing the mill, we continued down 6A and when Rachael saw the sign for Breakwater Road, she insisted on showing me the beach. Like many of the bay beaches the setting at Breakwater was idyllic—deep lush sea grass swaying in the gentle breeze—tidal pools formed as the tide recedes into the bay—attractive sand flowers with pastel colors caught my eye—gentle dunes shielded the soft sand of the beach—and the beauty of the seagull in flight was present to capture my imagination. It was the ideal place to sit with the perfect woman, and simply relish in her presence.

The day flew by and before we knew it we were heading home. I was encouraged by our conversation with Roisin, and frankly, upbeat over how natural and comfortable my relationship with Rachael was developing. It gave me the confidence to casually ask if she wanted to come over to my house to eat and hang out for the evening.

Rachael looked at me with her soft brown eyes, smiled and said, "That sounds like a plan, I'm starving. I'm sure your culinary skills on short notice are much better than mine."

"Early in my Navy career, I'd spent my share of time doing KP, "kitchen patrol." I peeled a lot of potatoes in the presence of excellent cooks who shared their talents with me. I hope that I can I live up to your expectations."

Rachael playfully winked at me and said, "Don't worry about it, you can always buy takeout since I made our lunch."

We made a quick stop at The Family Marketplace and bought chicken Kabobs, fresh vegetables, and wine. When we arrived at my place we were both famished. I fired up the grill and Rachael volunteered to take Sailor for a walk.

By the time Rachael returned, I had the patio table set, the wine poured, and added scented candles for ambience. While the little Casanova snuggled up to Rachael, I managed the grill. When the food was ready, I laid out the spread I'd been cooking for the two of us.

After finishing the meal and cleaning up, we returned to the patio and Rachael said, "Tell me about your favorite places you visited while in the Navy."

"Wow, I'll be honest, there were so many. It always seemed like the last place I'd visited became my favorite. Thinking about it though, I have a better perspective.

"I've crossed the Atlantic and been through the Mediterranean. We docked in plenty of wonderful old-world countries, but my favorite deployment was to the Pacific Ocean. My two favorite countries are Australia and New Zealand. During the time we spent in the area, I had the opportunity to take the train across the North Island of New Zealand from Auckland to Wellington. We toured Tongariro National Park with its three active volcanoes. My attraction wasn't limited to the natural beauty of the country. The food, vineyards, and the pleasant, friendly attitude of the people were very welcoming.

"Australia was a spectacularly beautiful country with warm, engaging people. We visited Sydney and had a wonderful experience. We toured the iconic Opera House, climbed the Harbour Bridge, and visited the Royal Botanical Gardens with the largest urban bat camp in the world. When I looked up into the trees, I saw these giant black balls. I asked a ranger about them, he told me they were actually bats. Needless to say, I hightailed it out of there before dusk set in and the bats came to life after sleeping all day."

Rachael and I shared a laugh as she said, "Smart man."

"When we left the city we headed to the Katoomba area of the Blue Mountain National Park. The day we visited the weather was perfect. The view of the Three Sisters, rock formation from the lookout at Echo Point was inspiring. Later, we grabbed a bite to eat at the Wentworth Falls picnic area and watched as mobs of kangaroos roamed freely. Some of these bouncing animals had a fur tone color of sandy-brown, while others had a rusty-gray. I couldn't believe how quick they were, I was reminded of the old "Road Runner" cartoon as they sped around the open field.

"But for me, the province of Queensland can steal your heart. We toured and hiked in Kuranda and Daintree Rainforests. The wildlife, tropical birds, mountains, waterfalls, and the forest with its deep green colors and a plethora of brilliant, colored tropical flowers were enchanting.

"The highlight of the trip was when we left the port in Cairns and headed out to the Great Barrier Reef where we spent the day snorkeling and admiring the colorful coral and tropical fish. A truly wonderful experience and one of the best days of my twenty-year Navy career."

"With all your wonderful travels, how did you end up staying on Cape Cod?"

"My first eighteen years were spent growing up in Southern California and a few days after graduation I headed off to boot camp. I've seen many places all over the world but hadn't spent much time learning about or experiencing our own country. So, when I walked out of the 32nd Street Naval Station in San Diego, I bought my truck and headed out to explore the country. I didn't really have a plan of where to go or what to see, but I had a good road atlas, and followed my whims as I crisscrossed the United States.

"I was driving on Interstate 90 heading to Boston to visit some of the historic sites when the sign for Cape Cod caught my eye. I'd read Thoreau's book, *Cape Cod,* a couple of years before I retired, so I just followed the road signs. The Town of Dennis looked to me about the middle of the Cape and a good basecamp to explore the entire peninsula. I made a decision to pull off Route 6 and stop at the first real estate agency I came across. That's how I met Kitten. She set me up in a small cottage near West Dennis Beach.

"I told you about the stormy night and how I found comfort on Cape Cod. I know it must sound odd, but it was the night I knew I belonged in Dennis, Massachusetts."

"You're a fascinating man Michael Maine," said Rachael as she leaned over and gave me a slight kiss on the lips.

Rachael had caught me off guard and before I could respond she gave me a longer kiss that really got my attention. Before things got too hot she said, "Let's take a romance slow Michael, we have a wonderful relationship and a very important investigation we're both committed to, but I've been wanting to kiss you for a long time."

My throat was as dry as Death Valley from the sheer joy I felt, and in the excitement of the moment, managed to eke out, "No more than me Rachael, no more than me."

"Well it's late, so why don't you drive me home and I'll let you give me a real goodnight kiss."

Okay, here's a secret, Rachael and I shared a beautiful goodnight kiss. One leaving me entranced, bewitched, mesmerized, captivated all verbs describing the intoxication I felt. I could hardly sleep that night, lying in bed imbibing the floral fragrance of Rachael's lips. I was as raptured by Rachael's kiss as a high school kid experiencing his first smooch. As if you're shocked when I tell you, "I'm truly in love."

The next day Rachael worked until six in the afternoon. I picked her up at the library and we headed over to West Dennis Beach. We walked a couple of loops along the mile-stretch of the paved lot. Afterwards, we strolled out over the jetty. The water of Nantucket Sound was relatively still with small, slow rolling waves. The air was warm, the sky showcased puffs of white clouds, and the reeds of the Bass River marsh stood upright with an occasional bend from a slight breeze.

It was a beautiful evening; the crowd had thinned out a while ago. I had thrown two beach chairs in the bed of the truck with a small table for our food. Tonight's menu included a cold supper of salad greens, assorted vegetables, and grilled chicken.

I'd been excited all day about this evening excursion with Rachael. I was looking forward to standing at the end of the jetty holding her hand. I wanted to convey to her how important this particular place was to me. My hope was that Rachel would feel the same energy I experienced every time I stood at the end of the stone, protector of the harbor. And also, share the same joy I felt when simply looking out over the water, gazing at the horizon.

As we stood holding hands at the end of the jetty Rachal said, "This is truly natures beauty in its simplicity. No wonder you found peace standing at the water's edge."

"Gazing at the ocean with its infinite vastness fills me with hope. Even though I'm minute in comparison, I feel like the early seafarers who departed from Palos de la Frontera with Columbus, as they ventured across the unknown with a belief they could accomplish anything."

"Standing here with you, I have the same hope. I truly believe our mission will be successful and we'll find the painting."

"I do too. It's more than hope, I'm always energized by the flow of the waves breaking against the rocks. Hope and energy drives me in our search."

"You're always full of surprises, Michael. I've been showing you the physical beauty of the Cape, while you're putting the majesty of what you see and feel into words. When I view the pristine splendor of nature in the future, I'm

171

going to look through the lenses of your eyes for inspiration. Thank you for a wonderful day."

We hung on the beach until the bugs came out, then packed it in. Rachael had to open the library in the morning, so it was an early night for the two love birds.

After dropping Rachael off at her car, and sharing an electrifying, goodnight kiss, it was back to the homestead for me. My mate was waiting by the door, and a shrill bark conveyed his disappointment when he didn't see Rachael.

"Pup, I already miss her too."

Sailor's lead was hanging from a peg behind the kitchen door, so I grabbed it, hooked him up, then headed outdoors for a walk. When we returned, I opened a Bud from the refrigerator and hung out with my little buddy on the patio.

It was a warm, starry night, and I enjoyed leisurely gazing at the dazzling beauty of the stars sprayed across the dark, night sky. As a kid, the first two constellations I'd recognized were the Big Dipper and the Little Dipper. I later learned they're technically not constellations, but part of the constellations known as Ursa Major and Ursa Minor.

In the Navy, when out at sea, I would find the time to head up to the main deck of the ship and observe the stars. There were many nights spent learning the identity of various star formations. Most of my favorites are the easiest to identify; Orion, the hunter; Taurus, the bull; and Gemini, the twins. I've seen my share of beautiful, late evening skies as the ship moved effortlessly, cutting through the night darkness and the ocean water. The rapid descent of a meteor or shooting star emitting a beacon of light as it quickly faded away was always a thrill. Most nights, my motivation was to simply enjoy the solitary quiet; recite the lyrics to the Willie Nelson version of *Let the Rest of the World Go By*. The soft melody of his twang, ringing in my head as I stared at the heavenly body above always brought me peace.

I admit, I love looking at the stars, but most of all, I'm star-struck over Rachael, as if you didn't know! To paraphrase the song writers, Ernest R. Ball and J. Keirn Brennan, under the "starry skies," we'll create a life of love and as the title says, *"Let the Rest of the World Go By."* I think Rachael has this ex-Southern California surfer pegged right, I am a romantic. A corny and over sentimental one at that!

Okay, I know some of you baseball lovers can't wait to find out if I strike out on a high fast one or hit a home run. But life, like baseball, is a pageant with its unique and individualized performances. As eager as I am to make a life with Rachael, remaining patient and not getting ahead of myself continued to be a daily struggle.

During the rest of June, Rachael and I had spent more and more time together. She was coming over to my house two or three times a week. My grilling skills continued to improve, and Rachael was always complimentary. I was hoping she was coming over for my company, and not simply for a delicious meal. See folks, that was my lack of confidence kicking in just now. Every time Rachael and I were together, she was fun loving, engaging, and playful. If I hadn't been so intimidated by her brains and beauty, we would probably have been a couple (or the adult version of going steady) by now. Keep in mind you ladies out there, most guys are like me, we're just plain scared when it comes to a woman. Many talk a good game but fold like an old-time accordion at the end of the day.

Now back to my story, we continued to focus on our search for the elusive painting without much luck. Before moving our search to Dennis, we made one final stop at Brewster Art. The gallery was an upscale, expensive, and showcased museum quality paintings, photographs, and sculptures. The day we returned to that bucolic town the weather was ideal. The sun was bright, not too hot, with a pleasant breeze off the water.

Entering the gallery was like entering one of the Smithsonian galleries of art. An elderly gentleman, tall, slim, and stately, who looked like he was dressed right out of a Brooks Brothers catalogue, greeted us. He was attired in a light-weight, blue blazer, gray slacks, white shirt, blue and red striped tie, and penny loafers. In a calm, casual tone he asked what we were interested in purchasing. Rachael and I teamed up to tell him our story as the dapper, art dealer listened intently.

"I met Rose only once. It was the day I went to her gallery to buy the Hartley Farm painting. A wealthy gentleman had called and said he was interested in purchasing it and asked me to represent him. According to his web page he's a benefactor of sorts. He would purchase artworks, and oftentimes, donate them to museums and various institutions around the country. Rose wouldn't sell, in fact, she wouldn't even let me see the painting. She intimated a distrust of my client, which was surprising, I'd never mentioned his name."

"Had you represented the client in the past?" asked Rachael.

"No, many times I never meet wealthy clients in person. We usually converse on the telephone."

"The painting wasn't on display?" asked Rachael.

"No, it wasn't. In fact, I later sent an associate to Rose's gallery and she denied the painting existed.

I asked, "Did she say why she wouldn't let your associate see the painting?"

"She made it clear, he wasn't the right buyer, and had concerns over the motives of my client. Rose somehow knew I was connected to this subterfuge. It was all very strange. She had an unusual affinity for the painting, almost religious. I represent art lovers, traders, benefactors, and yes, profit seekers. However, I'd never seen a reaction like the one I got from Rose."

"So, you wouldn't know if another gallery purchased it? asked Rachael.

"No I don't, I knew Rose was very sick and I don't want to sound callous. But, I wouldn't be surprised if she took the painting to her grave."

Rachael and I looked at each other with disbelief. We hadn't gotten the man's name, so I asked him for his business card. The name on the card read, Nathen Hartless, proprietor.

We thanked Mr. Hartless for his time, then left the shop. Once outside, Rachael said, "That was strange."

"Very much so, everyone else we spoke with had all praised Rose. Andrew and Rose had seen the painting, discussed it with Rose, and came away enchanted by it."

"Mr. Hartless does have a cold, business like persona. Maybe Rose didn't have a good feeling about him."

"Or the client Mr. Hartless never met or named."

"Michael, this is just another peculiar aspect of the case."

"I certainly hope Rose didn't literally take the painting to her grave as Mr. Hartless suggested."

"I have the same intuitive impression about Mr. Hartless as Rose. I suspect maybe she wanted him to think she would literally take the painting to the grave. I highly doubt that she did. Don't worry, we'll find the Hartley Farm painting."

"Rachael, I love your confidence. I'm not going to let Mr. Hartless discourage me. I agree, we will find the painting."

After the disconcerting exchange with Mr. Hartless, we took a break from our search and stopped to stroll around Drummer's Boy Park. A wonderful venue, with historical significance and natural charm. We enjoyed exploring Windmill Village and the centerpiece of the exhibit, the restored 18th century windmill. We then walked through the old Cobb House museum circa 1799. The Brewster Historical Society does a tremendous job maintaining the site and educating the public.

Rachael and I strolled out over the meadow-like field and sat on a faded, wooden bench with the allure of an Amish made loveseat. The two-seater was situated under the shade of a beautiful, old maple tree positioned near the grand gazebo. Our view from the crest of a small hill in the middle of the grassy public park was spectacular. We could feel the breeze off the bay as it penetrated a cluster of pines, shrubs, and other native trees separating the park from Cape Cod Bay.

I welcomed the serenity as a silence between us set in. I was learning from Rachael, oftentimes, simply being together, and not saying much, means more than words can express.

Rachael was the first to break the silence when she said, "Both of my parents died before I was thirty. My mother gave birth to me when she was in her early 40s, so I was an only child. I had a very good life growing up, but I always wished I had a sister and companion. My early years were spent in an adult world.

"When I was first married, I desperately wanted a family and for my children to have siblings, but it wasn't in my ex-husbands plans. I'm not trying to scare you away, and I don't know where our relationship will end up, but if I were to marry again—I would want a family. Before things get too serious, I needed to be honest with you."

Rachael's words brought this tough-guy sailor to tears. Listening to her speak from the heart about her desire for a family opened the closed, steel gates imprisoning memories of my past. Rachael's words exceeded my wildest dreams of where our relationship would end up. I immediately embraced her and when we separated, my teary eyes fixed on hers and said, "The two things that would make me the happiest man in the world is if we were to marry and have a house full of children."

I then gave Rachael a tender kiss on the lips and hugged her. She held the embrace and when we parted she said, "Because I've fallen in love with you Michael, it's important I have this conversation with you."

"I love you too Rachael, I've been smitten with you since the first day we met."

"Smitten, well you may be dating yourself Michael Maine. I hope you're not too old for me?"

"Don't worry darling, there's a lot of life and love in this old heart of mine."

After sharing a laugh, we both stood up, held hands, and headed toward the truck. The evening was setting in and

Sailor was anxiously waiting to take care of you know what, so we stopped off at my house to check on the little tyke.

Rachael asked if she could freshen up while I was taking the pup out for his walk. When I returned, I laid out his food. As I turned around, I walked into Rachael's arms and we kissed passionately. She gently took my hand and led me to my bedroom, closed the door, and dimmed the lights. There was enough illumination to take in the full allure of her body as we made beautiful love for the first time.

I would have given anything for Rachael to stay the night, but our impromptu rendezvous left her unprepared for work in the morning. With great reluctance, we left my warm bed in the wee hours of the morning and drove to her home. Rachael wouldn't get much sleep, but I was prepared to sleep most of the day in perfect bliss.

Life was great for me as we welcomed in the July heat and the start of the peak tourist season. Rachael loved the crowds and the influx of people from all over the world. She was extremely busy at the library, particularly on days when it rained. With inclement weather, the library became an attraction for the local kids, and those visiting and vacationing on Cape Cod. Rachael enjoyed seeing new faces, especially the youngsters with their passion for reading.

The invasion of summer visitors han't inhibited our investigation. In fact, I felt we were nearing the end of our search as we began visiting galleries in Dennis and Yarmouth. I may be obsessing, but a strong presence of Mary Hartley consumes me every day as if her shadow were a blanket covering me. She's been in my dreams and on nights when it rains, I often find myself laid out on the couch in my rain gear with Mary's spirit vivid in my mind.

Rachael and I carried on with our search, visiting numerous galleries, but without much luck. We did, however, have better success taking in the local landmarks. With Rachael as my guide, she would lead the way, while continually opening my eyes to the grandeur and natural scenery of the Cape.

One of our stops was to Gray's Beach in Yarmouth Port, a short drive off 6A. We walked the boardwalk that jetted out above the saltwater flowing from the bay. With each step we took over the solid, wooden planks the closer we came to the vegetation that makes up the salt marsh. Some of the plants were green, while others had the color of a Kansas wheat field. A variety of birds and seagulls were active in search of food. From the observation deck, we had a view of the clear water flowing around us. We watched hungry, native fish migrating to the area looking for a meal.

A silver-gray striper silhouetted by the sun's rays danced to its own rhythm as if an actor waiting for the audience to applaud.

My attention was drawn to a flock of seagulls that had descended toward the soft sand hunting for scraps of food left behind by beachgoers. A lone white bird, dove-like in appearance, broke from the pack, gliding toward Rachael and me. On closer inspection, it was merely an illusion of a dove. The figment was actually a pure-white seagull. As the bird moved away from us, heading west, soaring toward Barnstable, the bright sun shone a halo's glow over the gull.

"Michael, look how the sunlight is radiating off the seagull, how beautiful."

"My imagination was taken in by the purity of the color. I perceived the gull to be a dove, similar to the one in Meg's painting. Now, with the glow of a halo created by the sun, I wonder if the seagull is special and trying to communicate with us?"

"I'm beginning to believe you're the person Rose had been waiting for to buy the Hartley painting. You appear to have a special connection to Mary Hartley, and you see and feel things others don't."

Rachael's words sent a shiver through me, all I could say in response was, "We need to find the painting."

Standing at the end of the boardwalk with Rachael at my side enjoying the ecosystem of plant and migratory wildlife, while watching the mysterious seagull, made me realize it was time to make this wonderful woman my wife. We share so much in common, the love of reading, the outdoors, and a simple lifestyle; not to mention bedroom activities. Like you don't want more details in that department. This shy sailor will keep the bedroom door closed to you *Fifty Shades of Grey* lovers!

Before I could propose to Rachael, I needed to tell her about my life before I'd entered the Navy. I didn't want to have any secrets between us. For me, it would be very difficult. In over twenty years, I've never spoken to anyone about my first eighteen. I've kept everything bottled up inside of me; not that I haven't thought of those times on many occasions. It's a part of my life I've never shared with anyone. I needed to find the right moment to tell Rachael the story of young, Michael Maine.

\*

What started out as an optimistic month, July became a very frustrating period in our investigation. Dennis, Yarmouth and Barnstable had many galleries, none however, carried the type of art relevant to our search. The employees, artists, and owners of the various shops we spoke with had not heard of the Rose Gallery or the Hartley Farm painting. The hopefulness I'd felt seeing the mysterious gull had now faded into the past.

On the romance side, July was the best month of my life. Rachael, Sailor, and I had bonded in a way that convinced me we would soon be a growing family. However, with August fast approaching, my anxiety increased. I hadn't yet talked with Rachael about my past. Don't get me wrong, there were plenty of opportunities, but this tough guy, Navy man was sure his emotions would get the best of him and always turned chicken when there was an opportunity to tell Rachael.

To boost my courage, I thought I'd host a cookout and introduce Rachael to my small circle of friends. She was already acquainted with Kitten and there was an immediate connection between the two. I wanted her to meet my one real friend, Marco, and his partner Daniel. During my monthly visits to the interrogation chair, as she groomed my hair, I'd kept Sarah fully informed of the status of my relationship with Rachael. Since she knew so much about me and my girl, I included her. Rachael also invited a few friends and colleagues from work.

All in all, it was a fantastic night. The group mixed naturally, while I managed the grill. Rachael played hostess, and you know her, she has a natural talent for making people feel at ease. She got a big laugh from the gang when she told of how I enticed her to dinner with the promise of some home cooking. Rachael said, "Michael served me the most tender, delicious striper that Marco had caught, while the one he snagged went untouched."

Rachael and Sarah hit it off right away, exchanging tidbits of information about you know who. Sarah told Rachael she regularly embarrasses me when I go to the salon for my haircuts. She couldn't resist mentioning my school-boy enthusiasm for Rachael. My girl thanked Sarah for her artistry in making over my Navy regulation haircut into a stylish, contemporary look. They shared a laugh when Rachael said, "It was the haircut that won me over."

There was an instant camaraderie between Rachael, Marco, and Daniel. When I introduced the three to each other, Rachael thanked Marco for his friendship with me since I was so new to the Cape. Marco told her the Navy connection and shared experiences made bonding easy, plus I was a good guy and a great catch for her. Rachael got a laugh when she responded with a fishing phrase and said, "You know the fishing practice of "catch and release," well, when I caught Michael and tried to release him, he just kept coming back."

Hey folks, you know there's more truth to her statement than I want to admit. But, this fish wasn't giving up. Watching Rachael as she circulated amongst our guests, it really hit home how lucky of a guy I was to have landed on Cape Cod and found her.

Both Rachael and I spent time filling Kitten in on our search for the Hartley painting. Kitten with her upbeat personality was very encouraging, telling us she was sure we were getting close. Of course she kidded me and got a laugh when she said, "Michael, is there really a Mary Hartley and a painting or was that simply the greatest pickup line of all times?"

One last thing, and I'm sure you're all wondering, where was Sailor? Well the pup gave Rachael a run for her money in the war of hostess versus host. The little tyke was at his best, sucking up to our guests, basking in all the attention he got. He even edged out Rachael when she seemed to be winning the battle. The sneaky pooch would cozy up to her for some quick loving, then shoot off like a rocket to hog all of the affection he could get from our guests. Honestly, he was pretty much on his best behavior, just a glutton for more attention than a New York City street performer.

I was sad to see the night end. Everyone thanked me and Rachael for the great time they had. Sailor was their lucky charm, sitting by the door as solid as the Blarney Stone while people started to leave. Instead of a kiss, he got a pat on the head, as each departing guest repeated the same compliment, "You're such a good boy." Of course the big hambone ate it all up. Not easy living with a celebrity.

Rachael and I had finished cleaning up by midnight. Sailor was fast asleep after the last guest said their goodbyes. While we didn't get much sleep with our naked bodies passionately clinging together (that's it for details, folks), we both felt energized in the morning. When we awoke, we fast paced our routine, I went for a quick run, while Rachael gave Sailor some loving and a nice walk. She had him wagging his tail in no time. I was beginning to wonder whose dog the pooch was, but then realized, I'm going to marry this wonderful woman and that makes Sailor our dog. Marry this wonderful woman, now that's one great phrase!

We then headed out on our investigation. It didn't take us long to reach our destination from Dennis. We leisurely drove along 6A, passing through Yarmouth before entering into historical Barnstable. A town of seven villages, originally developed as a farming community. But, by the end of the 19ᵗʰ century, Barnstable was a hub of maritime activity. Magnificent sea captain's homes lined what was then called the Old King's Highway, now called Route 6A. Three former United States Presidents spent many summers vacationing in Barnstable. Among them were Ulysses S. Grant, Grover Cleveland, and the popular, John F. Kennedy.

While driving 6A, Rachael pointed out some of the great houses hidden behind hedges and shadowed by large oaks, maples, or walnut trees. Sprinkled amongst these grand palaces were smaller homes, restaurants, and shops. The galleries we visited teased us immensely. The artistry on display reflected much of the town's historical roots. There were paintings depicting the dichotomy of seafaring. These paintings ranged from the tranquil beauty, to the destructive waves of the Atlantic Ocean. Hundreds of nineteenth century portraits of farms lined the isles of several shops. The artist brush strokes on many of these paintings brought the artwork to life. Our optimism soared during the morning, by afternoon, we couldn't help feeling disappointed. The forty mile distance between Eastham and Barnstable brought us to the type of art we were searching for, but no closer to the Hartley Painting. The people working in the shops we visited had never heard of either the Rose gallery or the Hartley Farm.

Rachael and I refused to be discouraged by the results of our hunt and agreed to enjoy the rest of the day. After sharing a light lunch, our first stop was the Sturgis Library. Rachael wanted to show me the oldest building in America that is home to a public library. The centuries old, yellow house with a black, front door and shutters was built in 1644 and listed on the National Register of Historic Places. Rachael knew all the librarians on duty, and she beamed with enthusiasm as we toured the library and introduced me as her "Boyfriend." Of course, my beam was as bright a Sirius, the "Dog Star."

After leaving the Sturgis Library, our next stop was to the Audubon Society's Long Pasture Wildlife Sanctuary. The natural setting of this refuge can take your breath away. You can enjoy the beaches, walk the trails, or bird watch in one of the meadows. Eastern Red Cedar trees shade most of the trails to help keep you cool while the paths weave through the vast acreage of pristine greenery.

The Audubon property abuts Barnstable Harbor and sits opposite the headland, home of the Sandy Neck Colony. At the start of the Overlook Trail, a few wooden steps descend to a boardwalk cutting through a piece of the

Barnstable Great Marsh. Standing at the end of the short walkway, gazing to the left, moored boats sit idle, gracefully bobbing with the rhythm of the water. Across the inlet is the most spectacular view of the Sandy Neck Lighthouse at Beach Point. The grand, old structure dates back to the eighteen-twenties. Painted white, the tower is pictured against native shrubs and sandy dunes. The forty foot brick sentinel, adorned with a black top, stands tall at the point where the harbor meets the bay.

A short distance away is The Great Marsh Wildlife Sanctuary offering a number of trails for visitors to explore. Rachael and I spent the remainder of the afternoon moseying along the paths that bring you to the edge of the salt marsh. We were rewarded with some lively bird activity. A couple of Double-crested Cormorants landed nearby with a splash. We stood quietly and watched a Great Egret and Great Blue Heron slowly wade in the shallow water of the marsh. The only sound we could hear was the choir-like harmony of birds chirping. While I admired everything I was seeing, I'm disappointed in how little I actually know about what I enjoy most. Nature at its best; the lush greenery, the numerous wildflowers with distinct, warm colors, and the birds too numerous to identify. I wish I had been born with a bigger brain and the ability to retain all the names of the birds, flowers, and plants that make up the great marsh's ecosystem.

After spending a wonderful day in search of the painting, visiting the Sturgis Library, and exploring two of the Mass Audubon's pastoral sites in Barnstable, a tranquility come over me; and I knew before the day ended Rachael would know my full story.

By the time we arrived at my house, Sailor was ready for his walk. Rachael and I took him out and let him lead the way. He headed out in charge, it's the best way to make him believe he's the boss, and to tire him out. Once back at the house, Rachael sat outdoors on an Adirondack chair massaging her new beau, while I fired up the grill. Like I told you before, I occasionally indulge in a small portion of red meat, so I had marinated a steak for me and chicken for Rachael's salad. The smell of the food sizzling over the flames made my mouth water. To temporarily accommodate my taste buds, it was a red wine night for me, and Rachael had her glass of white.

When the meal was over and the cleanup was finished, we returned to our Adirondacks. The sun had started to fall and the evening colors began to change. I enhanced the aura with the click of a switch and the gas fire pit was glowing. There was a silence between us as we sat watching the flame. My mind was working overtime trying to start the conversation I'd been postponing for too long, when suddenly, the words began to flow.

"Rachael, you had asked me what my story was, and I told you about my Navy years. What I didn't tell you, and what I haven't spoken of in over twenty years, is my life before the Navy."

Rachael looked at me intently, as her soft eyes focused on mine. She gave me a warm smile and said, "I've been waiting to hear your story since we first met, whatever you have to say I'm here to listen. I love you with all my heart."

My eyes began to water, and it took me a few moments to regain my composure before I could talk. When I did open up, I said, "In the spring of my senior year, my family died in a car accident. They were on the way to watch me play my last game of high school baseball. Both my parents, younger brother, and sister were killed. I was the last person left on the field when the police showed up and broke the news to me. You can imagine the shock I felt when I was told. The school was very supportive, and my friends and their parents were wonderful.

"My parents built a successful business after moving to California, and we had a beautiful house and a wonderful life. All our relatives were from the Midwest, and we didn't have much contact with them. Several siblings of my parents I'd never met arrived for the funeral services and appeared to be very nice. Without really asking me if they could stay at the house, they sort of moved in. At first they were helpful with planning the services and handling the funeral arrangements. Once the services were over most of them returned to the Midwest, but a brother of my father and one of my mother's sisters remained. They said they wanted to assist me with sorting through the complexities of the estate.

"It didn't take long for me to realize what was going on and what their motivations were. I could hear the whispers between them and the long-distance phone calls to other relatives.

"I had thirty days until graduation. I had just turned eighteen, an adult under California law, and the sole heir to the family estate according to my parents will. Maybe these unknown relatives had my best interest in mind, but they didn't act that way.

"After an aggravating day of dealing with an aunt and uncle, I didn't really know at all, I knew I had enough. The next morning, I walked into the Navy recruiting office and signed a six-year contract. My enlistment would begin the day after graduation. I didn't want to stay in my house any longer with relatives who came across as self-serving. There were also the painful memories of my loving family that haunted me, so I rented a room at one of the local hotels. A close friend of mine's father was an attorney, and I hired him to create a trust fund and represent my interests until the estate was settled.

"Things moved expeditiously after my lawyer got to work. My aunt and uncle were evicted, and once the estate was probated, the house and business were put on the market for sale. I had plenty of cash from insurance and various bank accounts left to me, so money wasn't a concern. After all, I didn't need much, I was going to be employed by the Navy in less than thirty days. My lawyer wrote to me after the case was settled to tell me the relatives were laughed out of court when they argued that I was too young to manage the estate, and needed their guidance. It's a tough case to make when the person you claim needs guidance is wearing a military uniform and serving his country.

"The sad thing about the whole affair was I never really had the opportunity to grieve. I was smothered by these relatives I didn't know, and frankly, didn't care for. I had just lost my entire family at eighteen and was in shock. During the early years of my Navy career, I struggled coming to terms with the death of my family, and finally, I'd learn to compartmentalize my feelings. I have wonderful memories I keep close to my heart. Those experiences helped me deal with what happened and allowed me to move on with my life."

While the tears were flowing down my checks, Rachael was crying softly and through her tears, she said, "Oh Michael, I'm so very sorry for your loss and at such a young age. When my parents passed away, I was nearly thirty, and felt their absence for many years. Even today, there are times when I wish I could reach out, touch them, and talk with them."

"There were times early on when the loss was unbearable. One of the things the Navy does well is keep you busy, and never alone. Whether you're on duty, sleeping, or on your down time, you're surrounded by sailors, so the constant presence of companions made moving forward more bearable. Like I told you, I haven't spoken to anyone about my life before the Navy, while I'd thought it would be hard, telling you was one of the easiest things I ever did. It hurts to talk about the tremendous loss I still feel, but I love you, and telling you my story lifts a burden of secrecy I've kept locked up inside of me."

Rachael snuggled up to me and sat on my lap. She quietly said, "I love you Michael." As she kissed me gently; I squeezed her tightly.

We didn't make love that night, we remained tenderly fixed in the Adirondack chair. All we needed was the warmth of each other's body and the love we have for each other. I felt enormous relief talking with Rachael about my loss. I now realize how important it is for me to keep the memory of my family alive, not only in my thoughts, but also in my words. Through Rachael, I was able to talk about my family and share many of the happy times we had together.

That warm summer night during the waning days of July was the turning point in our relationship. I was hoping for a September wedding and planned to ask Rachael to marry me the first week of August. With no immediate family for us to consider, a wedding in thirty days didn't seem too difficult to pull off.

I've always loved the month of August. The days are long, the sun is strong, and the evening air begins to cool. Most early mornings are a pleasant time for a run, and that was exactly what I did to welcome in the eight month of the year. While running, my thoughts were of Rachael, and how easy it was for me to confide in her. She's an attentive and sensitive listener; she didn't need to say much. Rachael showed me her deep affection, by simply cuddling with me, and sharing my pain. I knew a marriage with Rachael would complete my life.

After returning from my run, I took the pooch for a walk and grabbed a quick outside shower. Hunger pains drove me to the Yellow Cottage for breakfast. Since my relationship with Rachael started to evolve, I'd avoided the local haunts. My life was centered around spending time and enjoying the company of Rachael and Sailor.

It was nice to see Ed, the cook, and shoot the breeze with him. We quickly got caught up on the local gossip. After a less than healthy breakfast, I made my way out to Harwich and tanked up my truck. As you already know, I try to get all my gas at Speed-A-Way because of my relationship with Marco. Even though it's still pretty casual, he's the closest I have to a real friend. Like I said before, he's a Navy man and we share similar experiences; plus he's a hell of a good guy.

After spending an hour with Marco shooting the breeze, I swung by D's to grab a coffee. Folks, is it only me? I just can't get used to calling double Ds plain, old D. Anyway, I continued to the library, I was dying to see Rachael. When I entered the main entrance and walked through the double doors, I was rewarded with a broad smile when my girl saw me. Her warm glow and twinkling eyes radiated love and made my day.

We arranged for me to pick her up at her house when she was through with work for the day. Since she had the next day off, Rachael planned to stay the night at my place. We committed to an early start so we could spend the day visiting galleries in the town of Sandwich.

With last night's conversation in the forefront of our minds, our passions were elevated. To the disappointment of the third wheel, Rachael and I made it an early, and mostly sleepless night, as we showered each other with love.

To make up for ignoring the pooch that previous night, the next morning good ole Sailor got his share of love from Rachael. Now I'm the jealous one!

While my girl took man's best friend for his walk (I'm beginning to wonder whether if there's any validity to the old cliché), I went for a quick run. It wasn't long before Rachael and I were in my truck cruising on 6A passing through Yarmouth Port, and heading toward Sandwich.

Rachael and I covered a lot of ground, browsing through the many art galleries located in the 380-year-old town. By two in the afternoon it was time for a break, so we headed over to the Town Neck Boardwalk. While we didn't have much luck finding the painting, we were fortunate enough to squeeze the truck into one of the few available parking spaces in the small lot.

After sharing a quick bite to eat, Rachael and I strolled over the 1350-foot wooden plank walk, the gateway to Sandy Neck Beach. As we reached the narrow, railless overpass across Mill Creek, my only thought was, I hope I don't meet Little John! After all, I wouldn't want Rachael to think I wasn't the better man.

While standing at the halfway point, we watched the incoming tide fill the marsh. As the water levels rose, the area surrounding the walkway became a highway of flowing streams. The lush greenery, indigenous of the salt marsh attracted flocks of native and migratory birds. These creatures of flight were soaring above, patrolling the wetland for nourishment. A pair of seagulls silhouetted against the blue sky diverged, as one performed an Olympic style, forward dive into the clear water, and ascended with a reward for his effort.

We couldn't help lingering on a pine bench with a quarterback's view of our surroundings. A vantage point that provided the comfort of a cool breeze. While the sleepy rhythm of the light air had the brownish, seagrass oscillating, my eyes struggled against the Sandman sprinkling dust.

Rachael nudged me awake before I had time to plummet into a dream-like trance.

We spent nearly two hours at Sandy Neck and were reluctant to leave. There were more galleries for us to visit before we left town, so we made our way to my truck. After visiting two art studios, we entered a third, called Elliot's Exclusive Artwork.

Entering the store, we immediately recognized the art as high quality and very expensive. Elliot approached us and introduced himself as the owner. From his gaze you got the sense he was sizing us up, trying to determine if we were buyers or lookers. He had an odd personality, formal, inattentive, and haughty. While we spoke, he let his head and eyes wander around the shop, appearing distracted. When he asked us to describe the painting, we gave him a general overview of what we believed the artwork would look like.

"An old farm, that doesn't sound very inspiring," said Elliot.

We ignored the comment and remained silent as he told us it wasn't the type of painting he would sell. Elliot seemed to remember hearing of something similar. Although, he couldn't recall anything more specific, but said, "You must be on the right track, because you're in the right town." With an aura of arrogance, he continued and said, "You can find anything in our lovely town or something nicer in my studio."

We couldn't wait to leave his store, so we thanked him for his time and praised the artwork in his shop. He invited us to come back to his gallery anytime and said, "I'm sure I can find a piece of art that you could probably afford to buy for the young lady…and it wouldn't be a picture of an old barn."

Again, we didn't respond to his comment. When our eyes met, Rachael and I shared a secret smile. We had seen the small, printed, price tags on the side of the picture frames. Prices that made the Hartley painting look like a bargain.

Sitting in my truck, our enthusiasm was waning. We asked each other, was Elliot simply full of bluster, or did he believe his words would somehow lure us back to his shop to purchase an overpriced piece of art? After nearly a six-month search, I would have liked to believe Elliot had provided us with hope; and that we were nearing the end of our journey. The words, nearing the end of our search was too disappointing to contemplate. I greatly relished the time and experiences I'd shared with Rachael in our pursuit for the painting; but finding the artwork and locating the skeletal remains of Mary Hartley was more important than the enjoyment of working together had provided us. I continued to have a strong, overwhelming obligation to ensure Mary gets the Christian burial she desired. Besides, once Mary was laid to rest, Rachael and I would spend our time creating new experiences and maybe even tackling another mystery.

The ride home to Dennis was relatively quick. The traffic on the Mid-Cape Highway tends to move at a pace greater than the posted speed limit of fifty-five miles per hour. Rachael and I remained mostly silent, we did voice our thoughts about Elliot's comments, "You can find anything in our lovely town," and "You're on the right track." He was also encouraging when he told us of hearing about a similar painting, but then flippantly, called it an old barn. After searching for over half-a-year, despite Elliot's obtuse manner, we wanted to believe we were nearing the end of our search.

We deliberately avoided mentioning his personality. I'm sure you all heard the old adage, and I'm paraphrasing— if you don't have anything nice to say about someone, don't say anything. You get my drift!

Rachael is too nice, but I'll level with you here; Elliot came across as a pompous donkey (I'm sure you know the real cliché).

I think the real reason we were quiet was there would be no repeat of last night's extra-curricular activity. We were playing the responsible adults. Rachael had to be up early to open the library in the morning. This honorable sailor wasn't going to guilt his lady, since the only thing preventing me from sleeping until noon was a love of the early morning and my current roomy. You got it, the loveable four-legged pooch; my ex-best friend and Rachael's new best friend! Yep, the little Benedict Arnold abandoned my ship and landed a beautiful lifeboat.

Rachael worked the eight-to-two shift at the library on Saturday, and when I picked her up, we headed over to West Dennis Beach. We planned to enjoy the remainder of the day, starting with a walk around the parking lot, and then taking in a little sun.

I'd been nervous all morning and you know why. Today's the day I'm asking Rachael to marry me. I'm confident she'll say yes, but I'm anxious, and frankly, still bewildered she's attracted to me. Like I told you before, Rachael's an obvious stretch on my part, but hey, one never truly knows the mystery of love.

The parking area at the beach was crowded, but the lot's big. I found an open space around lifeguard tower seven and backed the truck up against the wooden retaining wall. We walked on the marsh side of the lot, heading in the direction of the jetty. After making a couple of loops, I was sufficiently composed for the big moment. We sat on one of the wooden benches at the entrance of the jetty. We spent thirty minutes or so watching the boats return from a day on Nantucket Sound. With my courage up, we began to walk along the flat stones of the jetty, balancing our way to the end of the breakwater barrier. It was a familiar spot, and one that gave me confidence.

The large boulders that makeup the jetty are shaped like a flat, topped pyramid. The underfoot provides a solid foundation to stand on. As I dropped down on one knee, Rachael must have thought I'd lost my balance. She clutched my arms with Hulk-like strength to support me. This proposal wasn't going as planned. As I resisted her help, she slowly let loose the vice-like grip she had on me. When our eyes locked, I made my move with all the confidence of a male alligator being dragged underwater by its female mate and said, "Rachael, since I met you nearly a year ago, my love for you has grown more and more every day. But it was over these last six months, I've learned who you are as a person. I know your kindness, sensitivity, and the love you so willingly share. I foresee a wonderful life with you, a family, and growing old on Cape Cod, a place we both cherish. Rachael, I'm asking you to marry me and share the rest of your life with me."

Rachael slowly dropped to her knees and kissed me on the lips. She gave me a bear hug; the strength of her grip and the heat of her body were intoxicating. When she released me from her forever hold, she smiled broadly, and said, "Yes, Michael, I will marry you. I love you with all my heart and soul."

We spent the rest of the day hanging out on the beach, mostly smiling and occasionally sharing light kisses. The sun stood high over Bass River, so we positioned our chairs with Nantucket Sound on our left and the salt marsh on the right. I noticed a red-tail hawk flying over the grassy wetland and said, "Look Rachael, the Hawk, it floats in circles."

"Are you an astute observer or are you thinking of the poem, *The Marsh Hawk,* by Mary Oliver?"

"I love her poetry and her concentration on the quiet, beauty of nature."

"Michael, you truly are full of surprises. She's one of my favorite poets and I adore her poem, *Wild Geese.* It's a poem that can bring me to tears. What's your favorite?"

"*Why I wake early,* I had thought of it the first day of June. I'd gotten up with the sun and when I stepped outdoors, the rays were shining down on my face. At that moment, I thought of you. It's funny, I've been wanting to tell you about Mary Oliver's poetry since then, but for some reason it had slipped my mind. Today is such a special day, I'm glad I waited."

"I'm happy I know another one of your secrets, Mr. Poet Lover."

"I do admire poets and writers who can bring the natural world to life with their words. I think Mary Oliver is the true legend of the art."

"Did you know she lived on Cape Cod?"

"No, I didn't, where did she live?"

"She lived on the Outer-Cape, in Provincetown. A truly inspiring area of our wonderful peninsula."

"It's getting close to dinner time, so why don't we pack-up for the day. We can discuss more of Mary Oliver and her poetry on the way to my place."

When we arrived at the home front, Sailor was waiting and could sense there was an excitement between Rachael and me. The bouncing little critter got a hug from Rachael and a long walk down 6A to Bridge Street and a right onto Sesuit Neck Road. We sat at a wooden picnic table and ordered food at the Café on the Harbor. We had a view of the sun fading in the distance, while watching the weary boats returning from a long day on the water.

The walk back to my house gave us time to digest and for little tyke to get tuckered out. With my mate snoring softly and the bedroom door closed, we made love with a passion I never knew existed.

The next day was Sunday and Rachael had the day off from work. We had a leisurely day hanging out at the house and playing with the pup. We did make it to the jewelry store where Rachael picked out her engagement ring. She selected a beautiful platinum, three-stone diamond ring in a shared setting with three smaller diamonds on each shoulder. It was the perfect choice for her long, slender fingers.

My girl loves country music and since she was off on Thursday, I surprised her with tickets to see the Brothers Osborne at the Cape Cod Melody Tent. The two brothers, as expected, put on a fantastic show and had the tent rocking with more enthusiasm than a Friday night jamboree at Legends Corner. It was nice spending an evening listening to great music with the woman I love. It gave us a chance to unwind and not think about the search for the Hartley painting. While I was absorbed in the music, I couldn't help stealing glances at Rachael. She was stunning, dressed in a red, sleeveless, knee length calico print sundress, Nashville bought boots, and a western style, straw hat.

Rachael was working the next three days and had a busy schedule. After the show, we both resisted the urge to return to my place for what would amount to a sleepless night. While our goodnight kiss lingered for some time, Rachael was reluctantly snug at her place, and I headed to the ranch to hang out with Sailor and try to reclaim his loyalty. Good luck with that, the yellow Lab was as much smitten with Rachael as me.

\*

It seemed every time it rained and thundered at night I found myself on the couch. When I woke up around four in the morning the room was eerily dark. I didn't have my rain gear on, but my body was drenched, as if I'd been surfing in my clothes. The vividness of the dream became my reality; I thought it couldn't have been a dream; it was so tangible!

Lying on the sofa, I could hear the pooch's shallow breathing. I kept my eyes focused on the ceiling and tried to recall every detail of that night's encounter. I was standing on the Town Neck Boardwalk; the rain was coming down at a forty-five-degree angle. The wind was intense as if a Jet Stream descended to earth, muffling what sounded like a chorus of howling animals. The approaching thunder boomed with the pounding of a cannon and gave me a frigid chill up my spine. Fear overtook me when the wooden planks underfoot began to erupt in uncontrollable turbulence, as if I were about to be upended, and plunged into the abyss.

I've had my share of frigid weather in the Navy, but the coldness I felt nearly paralyzed me. I couldn't discern if it was cold or fear that left me immobilized. Maybe it was just a lot of both.

Suddenly she arrived, standing a short distance from me was a woman, ethereal, transparent, ghostly. Flashes of lighting illuminated her beauty. She said, "Michael, you know me, I'm Mary Hartley; you're so very close you need to come back. You've read my letter; you need to come back, Michael. Come back before it is too late. I feel the Old Man's presence!"

I couldn't respond, my teeth were chattering to the speed of a drum roll. Mary had an anxiousness bordering on hysteria. She kept repeating, "Come back, come back, come back before it's too late!" The hard rain was washing over me with waterfall-like fury. Mary's presence started to fade as the doleful wail of the wolf grew louder. There was a sudden ruffling in the reeds to my right; the thin-leaved plants began to part, a sullen, Grendel-like howl reeked the air. An inhuman figure appeared through the opening in the grass. It was covered in insects and carrying a shovel. An angry, harsh shrill rang out, "You will not interfere, you adulterer!" My feet were frozen; fear overcame me. A loud screech broke through the darkness and an all-white seagull charged the parting reeds. Loud, Kong-like steps sped away from me. Emerging from the grassy marsh was a white dove transfigured from the gull. As the dove approached me, it metamorphosed back into a magnificent white seagull. When I looked, Mary was gone, and so was the bird!

Still prone on the couch, these thoughts exhausted me. Chilled, I again dozed off, until finally falling into a restless sleep. When I awoke, it was to the wet, gooey slobber of Sailor licking my face. As my eyes began to open, I could see the brightness of the sun peeking through the windows. I needed to clear my mind and think about the events of last night. One of the ways for me to regain my equilibrium is to fire up a pot of coffee and take Sailor out for a long walk. A change of clothes came first, the walk second. My mate appreciated the attention. With the pup wiped out from an aggressive walk, I'd sat at the dining table with the hot, strong brew and contemplated the previous night's supernatural encounter.

I rewound the scene over in my mind as the strong, caffeine stimulant jolted me with the stinging vibration of an electric shock. I then started repeating Mary's words in my head until I could hear my voice reciting them out loud,

"Michael, you're so very close to me you need to come back. You've read my letter; you need to come back, Michael. Come back before it is too late! I feel the Old Man's presence!"

I didn't fully understand her message, what was she trying to tell me? What did the freakish voice mean when he yelled, "You will not interfere, you adulterer!" Was the grotesque figure with the shovel Old Man Hartley?

I knew it all had to be a dream, but everything I experienced argued otherwise—the vividness of Mary's spectral presence—the sound of her voice and her fear—the rabid animal howls—the cold wet chill—the grating words of a distorted, demon-like figure—the fear that had engulfed me—and suddenly, the appearance of the white knight, the transforming seagull.

My thoughts stayed focused on Sandwich: Had we missed something? Was there a gallery we failed to locate? Elliot had been cryptic, saying we could find anything in Sandwich and something better in his store. Was it simply a sales pitch? Had he been duplicitous? Was there a more hopeful message in his words than we credited him for? So many unresolved questions made the dream, or out-of-body experience unsettling. I was sure of one thing, I needed to return to Sandwich as soon as possible.

I took a marathon of a shower, running the water between hot and cold. Once my head cleared, I could feel the tension in my muscles dissolve as if I'd spent an hour on a masseuse's table. Refreshed, I then headed over to the library. I wanted to catch Rachael on her lunch hour.

While my girl was surprised to see me, she gave me a warm welcome, and snuck me a quick kiss. The wait until she was free for lunch was short. We went outside and sat on one of the stone benches lining the front walkway. Rachael ate her food while I calmly relayed the events of my dream, metaphysical voyage, or whatever it was that had transpired.

At first I thought Rachael would think I was delusional, but like I said before, she's an open and attentive listener. Her warm, sensitive eyes told me she believed what I'd said, and felt what I'd experienced was more than just a dream. She said, "Michael, you have a strong transcendental connection with Mary Hartley. It's not easily explained in a rational manner, but nonetheless, it's very real to you."

Rachael's response warmed my heart, and her next comment made my day when she said, "Pick me up after work, around four, and we'll drive over to Sandwich. You heard Mary's frantic plea; you need to get back there as soon as you can. And, since we'll be in Sandwich during supper time, I'll let you treat me to a good, seafood meal."

"Rachael, when we find the painting, we may be too excited to eat."

After giving Rachael a strong embrace and a quick kiss, I headed over to my house. I took my partner for another walk to wear him out. My hope was that the search would be successful, and I would be home later than usual. The rambunctious critter enjoyed the extra exercise and attention. When I left the house Sailor was rolled up on the couch.

I was heading into the library as Rachael was walking out of the front door. I've grown extremely fond of my fiancée's place of employment. There's a great staff of professional librarians ready to assist you. The building is warm, intimate, and offers a full range of services. If you're looking for a quiet place to hang out with a good book, head over to number five Hall Street. You won't be disappointed.

Looking at Rachael as we approached my truck, I could see she was as excited as I was to return to Sandwich. She may have been interested in the seafood as much as the search, but my instinct was telling me, tonight we'll find the painting of the Hartley Farm.

The traffic was light as we made our way down 6A. When we entered the Town of Sandwich, Rachael took out her notebook and began to check off the shops we'd already visited. We made our way past Town Neck Road and headed toward the Cape Cod Canal. There were plenty of galleries on the way, plus, there's a great fish restaurant right by the water with a captivating view of the canal and the adjacent marina. I owed my girl dinner, and to be honest, I was pretty hungry too. We sat at the window counter next to the bar and shared a salad topped with lobster. We had a terrific view of the canal and the myriad of boats harbored in the marina. The restaurant service was quick and we didn't linger. We still had two or three hours before the galleries closed and I was anxious to make the best of it.

After a few unproductive stops, we were nearing Town Neck Road when Rachael noticed a sign for the Sandwich Glass Museum. She knew the museum was closed, but recalled, when visiting last fall, seeing a variety of shops nearby. She couldn't remember if there had been an art gallery but knew there were small touristy type businesses in the area of the museum.

I made a right turn and followed her directions; I trusted Rachael's intuition. My thoughts return to Mary, her letter in the glass jar and the museum's proximity to the Town Neck Boardwalk. Was there a connection, I wondered; glass jar—glass museum? I wasn't sure what Mary meant when she said, "You're so very close you need to come back." The museum's not far from the boardwalk and the glass jar was the impetus for the investigation. Was that what she meant by being close to her? I couldn't figure out if these were signs and Mary was showing us the way, or if I was simply letting my imagination control my wishful thinking.

We searched the area around the glass museum, drove Main Street in the direction of the canal, then turned around and headed the other way. As we passed the Burgess Museum, a popular location exhibiting art, culture, and wonderful gardens, Rachael noticed a small shop on a poorly lit, side street bordering Main and 6A. As we approached the building, I noticed an all-white seagull poised atop the shop's sign. I gave Rachael a soft, discrete nudge and pointed toward the bird, but the seagull had disappeared.

When we pulled up in front of the store, we could see a variety of artwork visible in the window. The name of the shop was The Wishing Well, an odd name for an art gallery. Reading the words on the sign, I made a quick wish. Suddenly a woman's voice, I couldn't immediately recognize, was speaking in my head. As she spoke my heart began to pound. She said, "Your perseverance is rewarded, the search for the painting is over!" Startled by her telepathic statement, I asked myself, "Could we have arrived at our final destination?"

As I opened the door, a round, wood framed stained glass oracle, with a clear outer circle and a deep-blue inner circle held a white dove; its wings fully spread, graced the front entrance. A rising wave of tension filled my body as we entered the unique shop. Rachael admonished me to stay calm. I immediately reached for her hand to tap into her tranquil demeanor and maintain my equilibrium.

As we stepped through the front door, the air was filled with the aroma of burning incense. The fragrance radiated an alluring fruity, flowery scent. There were several vases of the now familiar red, white, pink, and yellow roses. The interior of the store was small, and the artwork on exhibit alluring. The quaint shop showcased much more than paintings. There was an assortment of statues made from various mediums, surrounded by bowls with sage, crystals, oracle and tarot cards, moon magic posters, and scented candles. The lighting was dim, and the combination of incense with the esoteric products created a mysterious, and mystical atmosphere.

A short elderly woman, slim, wearing a multi-colored Kaftan style dress came out of a room in the rear of the store and said, "I was closing up for the day, but take your time. If there's something specific you're looking for, I'm always able to help."

Rachael introduced herself to the woman and said, "We're looking for a painting of a farm, specifically the Hartley Farm."

The woman identified herself as Rose, causing both Rachael and I to quickly exchange glances. Her face was familiar, but her features were unmistakable. I nearly asked, if her last name was Flynn or if she'd owned a gallery in Eastham, but hesitated, not sure if I was ready for her answer.

Rose said, "I know the painting well, it's a possession I've had for many years. It's a wonderful rendition of an 1860s farm. The artist's brush strokes, with an interesting blend of historical colors combine to really bring the painting to life. I don't always have it on display, and to be honest, I'm not sure it's for sale. I may not want to part with it at any price.

"I love the painting so much; I often sit quietly and just admire it. The artist captured something enchanting, it's as if the artwork comes to life and has something to tell you. A strong force holds your gaze, sizing you up, deciding whether to speak to you. It's as if his creation is looking through you. I know it may sound strange and dramatic, but it really is captivating."

I introduced myself to Rose, told her of our search, and the motivation for wanting to purchase the painting. My words flowed as if someone else was speaking. Once the verbal spigot was opened, I relayed all of our experiences. Rose didn't flinch when I told her about the Mason jar, the letter, my ghostly encounters, and Mary Hartley's request. Rachael shared more details of our long hunt to find the painting.

After exhaustively telling our story, Rose said, "I've often known, looking at the painting, the artwork was calling out for the right buyer. While I love the painting and it will break my heart to part with it, I never thought I was the person the painting was calling out to. When I acquired the painting, I was told, 'You are now its guardian.' I didn't fully understand the meaning of my responsibility, but now I do."

Rose once again paused before speaking. She lowered her eyes, and we all remained quiet. A spirituality pervaded, as if she had asked for a moment of silence. When she looked up she asked, "Would you like to see the painting?"

Rachael and I simply nodded. I silently whispered, "Could our search really be over?" A quick glance at Rachael told me what I already knew, we were both dumbstruck.

Rose lead us to the rear of the shop, and behind a dark curtain separating the two rooms, the painting of the Hartley Farm was staring directly at us. My gaze was transfixed, a force held my eyes  intently on the painting. My body

218

twitched, I could feel a gentle rubbing of my skin, and then the presence of warmth caressing my heart. I was captivated by the feeling, hoping I was worthy, hoping the painting would talk to me.

The powerful sensation suddenly evaporated. I could hear Mary's voice saying, "Michael you're so very close to me, you need to hurry. Oh please Michael, time is running out! I feel the Old Man's presence!"

I longed for the warm feeling to return, but my mind was consumed by Mary's words. What did she mean? The painting stood before us, we found it. What of the Old Man's presence? I could hear Rachael's voice in the distance. When she got my attention she said, "Michael, look at the name of the artist."

I approached the painting with caution. Looking down at the bottom right corner was the artist's signature, written in a neat clear script was *"Michael Maine."* Seeing my name spelled out on the Hartley painting sent a quiver though my body. I felt the same weakness when I learned of the death of my family.

Rachael reached out and took my hand, the physical contact was reassuring. The love we have for each other steadied my nerves. I refocused my attention on the cursive script that spelled out my name. The signature was definitely not mine; the penmanship was much superior to my own. There was a graceful, artistic flow I simply couldn't replicate.

Rose broke my concentration when she asked, "Is the artist a painter you're familiar with?

"It's the name, Michael Maine, the same as mine. I'm certainly not the artist but the coincidence is startling."

"Could the artist have been an ancestor of yours?" asked Rose.

"I wouldn't think so; my family is originally from the Midwest and my parents raised me on the West Coast. My knowledge of relatives and family history is very limited."

"Michael, ever since you found the letter, you've had a strong connection to Mary Hartley. I don't believe there's a logical explanation for many of the unusual or mystical experiences we've encountered while searching for the painting. Your name inscribed in a 150-year-old masterpiece is certainly the biggest one," said Rachael.

Rose seamed unphased by what she was hearing. She had a warm smile and the look of one who was expecting me to walk into her shop at closing time. She said, "I see the passion you have for finding the painting. Your search for it alone is a testament to your commitment. I was told, one day the right buyer would come into my shop after a long journey. A voyage fraught with supernatural experiences, as if challenged to the test of "Gawain" Knighthood. Maybe you're the person deserving of the painting."

Rose then paused, and after what seemed like time moving like a snail on holiday said, "You're such a lovely young couple, and the painting is so expensive. If you're sure you want to purchase it, I'm willing to sell it to you. I felt the force of the painting; I know you're worthy. All that you have expressed to me, is a testament to your knighthood qualities of chivalry and loyalty. I'm confident you will hear what the painting has to say and find what there is of Mary Hartley. I don't think I could rest in peace until her soul was given a proper burial."

For several moments my mind raced. I had so many jumbled thoughts, as if my head was a pouch containing one-hundred Scrabble letters being shaken. What was Rose's connection to Mary Hartley? She had only heard today of Mary's letter, and her desire for a Christian burial. How could she say she wouldn't be able to rest in peace until Mary's soul was given a Christian burial? Did she already know about the letter? Mary's request? How could she know? What of knights, chivalry, and loyalty? Had she felt the same force from the painting that I had? Who is this Rose from The Wishing Well?

As I tried to calm myself, another thought entered my mind; Rose Flynn had expressed those same exact words to her great-granddaughter, "I don't think I could rest in peace until Mary's soul was given a proper burial." This realization jolted me with the same intensity I'd experienced the first time I jumped into the icy, frigid water off of a twenty-five-foot training tower.

The tornado whirling in my head swiftly dissipated when Rachael elbowed me back to reality. The lights in The Wishing Well had started to dim. Rose's skin tone began to gray, her face thinning, and her wrinkles deepening. She had a look of total exhaustion. It was as if her guardianship concluded, and suddenly, death was fast approaching. I held my questions as a fog like film permeated the shop preventing me from seeing Rose's shrinking persona. After writing a five-digit check, we extended our thanks to her. As we walked out onto the sidewalk, I could hear the door latch lock, as the lights in the small gallery suddenly went dark.

"What a wonderful woman," said Rachael.

"Did you notice her words, her physical change?"

"I hadn't noticed."

Rachael's response wasn't fully unexpected. So much had happened to me since I first found the Mason Jar that can't be explained. What had transpired in The Wishing Well was another experience I'll try to sort out in due time.

As I looked up, the night sky was a fabric of sparkling lights. Not a sound was heard; there were no wolf-like wails, Grendel-like howls, or Kong-like steps. There was no insect covered, devilish old man. There was no seagull or dove. There was simply a solemn peace and tranquility, pushing my scrambled thoughts into the deep recesses of my mind.

We had the painting of the Hartley Farm, our map to discovering the location of Mary's skeletal remains. I was relieved that the search for the painting was over. I knew our mission was only half complete, but those concerns were for tomorrow.

# 4

The painting had been securely wrapped by Rose, and I left it that way until Rachael and I could examine it together. Rachael had to open the library in the morning, and she thought it was best to go home and try to get a good night's sleep. I had hoped Rachael would stay at my place and help calm me down. I was still wound up, well past midnight, when I crawled into bed.

All I could think about as I laid awake was how far we'd come in solving the Hartley mystery. But, until we actually recovered Mary Hartley's remains doubt would plague me, and I slept the sleep of the burdened.

My mind was absorbed with the events of the last twenty-four hours. I couldn't separate fact from fantasy. Everything that had occurred to me seemed both concrete and factual: standing on Town Neck Boardwalk in the frigid rain; listening to the guttural sounds of howling animals approaching me; the crack of thunder and the sensation that the wooden planks underfoot would shatter, sending me into the abyss; the strange appearance of the chameleon-like seagull rescuing me from the horrid figure who had emerged from behind the parting reeds; the arrival of Mary Hartley with her pleadings, telling me over and over, "You're so very close you need to come back." The sound of her voice suggested that her anxiety was driven by fear. She implored me saying, " You need to come back before it is too late, I feel the Old Man's Presence," these were words that haunted me.

Then there was the mysterious gallery with the elderly shop owner, and the fourth elusive character with the name Rose. Seeing the words "Michael Maine" written in the corner of the mysterious painting chilled me through the marrow. All of these occurrences danced in my head and combined for one long, sleepless night.

At some point, I dozed off, and when Sailor's bark interrupted my slumber, I woke to a warm sunny day.

Despite the lack of sleep, I had extra pop in my step. I brewed coffee and took my buddy for his morning walk. After returning, I drank a quick mug of dark roast and headed out for a long, hard run. Returning, I rewarded myself with an extra-long, outside shower.

I wanted to keep busy until Rachael was through with work, so I took care of my neglected chores and ran some errands. The four-legged king of the house was riding shotgun in my truck. Like most dogs, he loves to have the window down with his head hanging out of the glassless opening, enjoying the refreshing breeze billowing around his face.

When we arrived at the library to pick up Rachael, Sailor immediately jumped in the rear passenger area of the truck. My first mate (I'd demote him to second mate, but he's the only mate I have), knows he was just borrowing Rachael's seat, and he was content to let her have it. Personally, I think he would rather have Rachael drive, while he rode shotgun with me sitting in the bed of the truck. (see parentheses above).

After arriving at my house, Rachael and I unwrapped the painting and laid it on my bed. A familiar, silent voice that I hadn't immediately recognized was telling me to turn the painting over. Without hesitation I told Rachael that I needed to lay the painting face down on the bed. She eyed me curiously, didn't comment, and assisted in turning it over. My eyes surveyed the white, unpainted side of the canvas, and then the wood frame. There was nothing visible to see, or feel, as I gently ran my hand across the rear of the painting. The same voice again played in my mind, and I now recognized it as similar to my own, said, "Warm the back of the painting with a candle. Use caution, start six inches away and move closer as words and numbers are revealed." I retrieved a candle from a cabinet in the kitchen and lit the wick. Rachael held the painting upright as I slowly moved the candle to and fro following the instructions of the spectral voice.

The first thing I noticed was the appearance of some sort of markings. There was nothing immediately legible. As the area warmed, a type of notation started to appear. When completely visible, inscribed on the canvas was a simple legend. The numbers and letters were written in the same neat script as the signature on the front. With a huge grin on my face, I showed Rachael the code written on the back of the painting.

"How did you know there was invisible writing behind the painting, Michael?"

"Rachael, a voice I couldn't quite recognize at first, was giving me instructions. The sound I heard became familiar, it was like I was telling myself where to look and what to do."

"Well, you're definitely the person the painting had been waiting to speak too, and you heard and understood its message."

I wanted to respond, but I wasn't sure what to say. We both knew there were way too many unexplained happenings associated with the Hartley's and the painting.

Our discovery showed the artist had paced off the distance between the house, two barns, a shed, four full-size trees, a large boulder, and two points from a stone wall delineating my property line. Most likely, he used a compass or protractor to determine where differing points intersected in order to capture precise locations and distances. We took our time studying the depiction of the farm and the corresponding legend. It became clear to us that the artist had painted the farm to scale.

We went outdoors to compare the lay of the land between now and the 1860s. Our objective was to find the location of the shed where Old Man Hartley had been furiously digging. We knew nearly everything had either washed away or was destroyed in the Saxby Gale.

When I first purchased the house, I noticed the remnants of an old fieldstone wall running along the rear of my property. From the painting, we now knew the wall was a barrier separating the planting fields from the more domestic part of the farm. The fertile farmland had washed away and was consumed by the salt marsh lining Sesuit Creek.

After identifying the location of two landmarks used by the artist, we were hopeful we could solve this puzzle. To locate the shed all we needed to determine was the intersection of two lines using the fixed points identified in the legend.

One remaining marker was a large, red oak tree nearly 170 years old. The aging, sturdy oak had miraculously survived the Saxby Gale. There's an aura of dignity, spirituality, and purpose to the big tree, like Grandmother Willow in *Pocahontas.* Another marker was a large, weatherworn boulder imbedded deep into the soil, its crest rose four feet high, and the sides were bruised and chipped like the stones of Pompeii.

The old tree brushes up against the scattered remnants of the crumbled stone wall and shades part of a small patch of fertile land that had been used for domestic gardening. The boulder was well away from the stone wall and sits on the left side, while the red oak stands on the right and a greater distance from the rear of my house.

Rachael and I used a compass to exact the angles from the fixed markers as delineated by the legend. The boulder was fifty degrees, and the tree was seventy and a greater distance to the shed. Individually, we paced off the distance from the landmarks; 125 from the boulder, and 250 from the tree. We kept our strides consistent with each other, and independently, we reached the same conclusion. The shed would have been located a short distance beyond my patio, and based on its size, a corner edged up to the spot where I'd found the Mason jar.

As I stood over the location where I had discovered the letter, I now knew what Mary meant when she said, "You're so very close you need to come back." I couldn't help thinking, where was the Old Man's remains? Mary's fear that she could feel his presence frightened me. I thought, was there a chance that somehow his ghost could interfere with Mary's wish for a Christian burial?

Rachael must have come to the same realization and said "Michael, Mary most likely died with the jar in her hands; her skeleton could very well be close to the patio. Your patio was surely built in the area where the shed once stood."

I would have liked to have picked up a shovel and started digging. However, forensic excavation is a delicate, time consuming process; particularly when trying to recover the remnants of a 150-year-old skeleton. We needed trained, professional forensic investigators to conduct a proper search if we were going to avoid desecrating the ground where Mary laid.

Rachael and I knew it would take time to arrange for an archaeological dig. In the meantime, we wanted to protect Mary's unholy tomb, so we placed a granite, Irish Cross where we believed her remains laid. We weren't taking any chances with the menacing wanderings of the phantom spirit of Old Man Hartley. Mary's warning that she could "Feel the old man's presence," still concerned me.

\*

Nearly six weeks passed from when Rachael and I concluded that Mary Hartley lay just beyond my patio. We had little success in getting the local authorities to expend the resources needed to recover Mary's bodily remains. I offered to pay for the entire cost of the excavation; I wanted forensic experts to respectfully recover whatever fragments of Mary they could. Money wasn't the issue, it seemed to me that politics and protecting reputations were the main obstacles.

Rachael still had connections with the FBI, so she reached out to her contacts after we failed to convince the local investigators that Mary Hartley, a victim of the Saxby Gale, was buried a short distance beyond my patio. I couldn't fault the local government; our evidence was thin and our story inconceivable. Bringing in additional officers for security and a cadaver dog would require police department resources; an expensive endeavor. There would be media attention along with the usual crowd of onlookers. Public interest would create a mini-circus and police and canine reputations would be at stake. Fortunately, Rachael's contacts came through and the experts agreed to dig up my yard.

The night before the search, Rachael made plans to meet her former colleagues in Boston and drive to the Cape with them in the morning. I was hoping to get a good night sleep and be at my best when they arrived.

As I previously mentioned, before I got involved in the Hartley Farm, I was a sound sleeper and rarely an uneasy one. But that night, as I lay in bed, my mind was restless, and my body was tossing and turning. It was as if my physical being was transported to another dimension. I felt like an icicle melting with cold moisture seeping from my body; Mary Hartley's letter weighed like an anvil sitting on my mind.

I'm not sure what time it was, but I could hear Sailor barking in the distance. Suddenly, I could hear the roar of Niagara Falls; the great intensity of the rain coupled with hurricane, force winds. The lightning, like flashes of daylight, lit up the sky, and the thunder, exploding with the force of a 16-inch gun mounted on a Navy battleship rocked my house.

I could hear Mary talking while she was writing her letter—*The rains started & the wind is blowing hard.* I could now see what I was hearing—*The Old Man is acting strange he is quoting scriptures about the end of the world.* Mary was looking at me, she was trembling as if caught in a frigid breeze, her words penetrating, she was so frightened—*I am afraid, he is outside digging around the shed between the barn & the house. He has been ranting & raving about a burial plot. I am so scared I'm not sure what he will do. He came into the house wet to his bones quoting Matthew about angels & heaven & not knowing when. Now Luke about the sun & the moon & roaring seas with waves people fainting with foreboding of what is coming.*

I watched the lunacy of the old man as Mary continued to speak—*He is now back outside the wind & rain keep coming we lost some trees & now the roof is off the shed. The Old Man is screaming & chanting I can't hear what he is saying I barely see him with the rain pouring down. He is back in the house & I hardly recognize him. He is yelling telling me the Lord is coming like a thief in the night.* I was witnessing the earthquake like destruction—*The house is shaking the roof has torn away & water is flowing into the house.*

I tried to talk to Mary but couldn't get her attention—*We lost the shed it washed away. The Old Man keeps shoveling I'm so afraid. If I should die tonight I beg for a Christian burial for I am a Catholic my soul needs a home*—I yelled to Mary, "I'll help you, I'll help you!."

*The barn is gone we lost the windows the house is breaking apart*—I saw Mary's world crumbling. *The Old Man is back I don't recognize him for he is in a rage. He is screaming Matthew 24, & Armageddon he said the end of the world is at hand. The Old Man just ran out of the house he is digging with a fury*—Mary, with deathly fear in her eyes, stared right through me. *I am putting this letter in a mason jar I beg for a Christian burial & absolution for my sins if I should die this night*—*Michael, you're so close don't give up, please don't give up. I fear the Old Man's lunacy*—I heard myself yelling, I'll never give up, I have the jar, I have your letter!

When I awoke, I found myself stretched out on the couch looking up at the painting Rachael and I had hung over the mantel. It hadn't immediately registered with me that the frame had completely decomposed, and the painting was gone. I was soaking wet, and my feet were heavy. I looked down and saw I was wearing my rubber boots. My foul weather gear was wet and wrapped in a ball on the floor. I thought it must have rained pretty hard during night. In my fatigue, I dreamt of the night of the Saxby Gale. The dream was so vivid, it left me disconcerted; the Ghost of Mary Hartley, and the raging of Old Man Hartley left me feeling like I was a witness to the horrible events of 1869.

Next to the couch, the pooch was snug in his pillowy bed. His body stretched out with his head resting against the soft side. My little buddy was in a deep slumber and completely content. Unlike his skipper, who was cold, wet, and had a hell-of-headache. I could see the early September sun blazing through the window shades as sunlight reflected off the hardwood floor. There was a stillness in my house and I thought, how quiet it often is after a storm. With my rubber boots still on, I walked outside, and immediately noticed how dry everything looked; not even morning dew was on the grass. I checked the weather APP on my phone and was stunned to learn it hadn't rained at all.

I couldn't get Mary Hartley out of my mind. What I watched replayed in my thoughts: the severity of the storm, the disintegrating Hartley Farm, the irrational behavior of the Old Man, and most of all, the pleading of Mary Hartley. She was trembling as she looked past me; I was yelling to her, I have the jar, I have the letter!

Suddenly, I realized the time, Rachael would be here in an hour with her FBI friends, the cadaver dog, and the local police. When I turn toward the house, Sailor was at the back door. He had a quirky look on his face, he seemed to recognize the skipper was acting strange. I opened the door and he was outdoors in a flash, I knelt down and hugged him and was comforted. Sailor returned the affection lavishing my face with gooey slurp. Relaxed I headed inside and grabbed a towel. In a flash, I was taking a shower with the water spraying hot, lightly burning my skin. The steaming water soothing. Once more, I ran the previous night's events through my mind; I had asked myself, "Was it real? Was it a dream? Had I somehow been transposed back in time to witness the horrific events of 1869?" Mary Hartley's pleas filled my ears like an echo in the chamber of a great canyon.

"The painting!"

I raced through the house and into the living room to examine the wall above the mantle. The beautiful wood frame and painting had rotted away and laid in a pile of grimy specs of dust on the mantle. I couldn't comprehend what I was looking at. My body was shaking, the towel wrapped around me had slipped off. I was standing naked in my front room. A chill brought me back to the present; I picked up the towel and covered my essentials.

The clock was ticking, so I rushed to the bedroom dressed in a pair of Khaki pants, boat shoes, a U.S. Navy tee-shirt, and a worn jean jacket. I brewed coffee hot, black, and stronger than usual. As I poured the dark liquid into my mug, I could see Rachael outside with the FBI agent. The handler with the cadaver dog, a large brown and black German Shepherd, was close by. The FBI forensic vehicle was parked in front of my house with the local police.

Trying to regain my self-control, I put the decomposed Hartley painting in the back of my mind. I needed to focus on the present. Telling Rachael about the painting would have to wait.

It didn't take long for the media to arrive and a crowd to gather. The local police did a good job maintaining security, and the professionals went to work at full tilt.

As I stepped out of the house, in a flash, Rachael was by my side, she gave me a smile and a quick, gentle kiss. She was focused, serious, and appeared nervous. She'd called all her contacts before an old friend went out on a limb to help her. He knew her reputation, but still, there was a lot of pressure because of the cost, and the publicity of an investigation involving the excavation of a 150-year-old person who had died in 1869.

I knew something of cadaver dogs from the Navy. They're expensive to purchase and too extensively train. They have a scent, one-hundred to one-thousand times greater than a human and can detect decaying body parts hundreds of years old. Odor rises from the soil and the cadaver dog sniffs for decomposition of tissue, blood, and bones.

Rachael introduced me to Thompson and Woodard, the two FBI special agents. Woodard put her dog, Fenway, to work immediately. She took off his leather lead and posthaste, with the concentration and intensity of a soldier in combat, Fenway was tackling his preferred duty. Agent Woodard was standing close by on the patio, while Thompson watched the canine from the side of my house. He would occasionally move to the front of the house to monitor the crowd.

Rachael and I sat on the top of the picnic table holding hands with our feet resting on the bench. She looked stunning in tight jeans, a white top, and a burgundy leather jacket. Her dark hair and dark colored eyes made her look very seductive. I wanted to forget all about the cadaver business and whisk her into the bedroom, but unfortunately, that would have to wait.

At this point, there was no option for a U-turn, it was full speed ahead. It took us nearly six months to find the painting in the storage room of The Wishing Well. Purchasing it was easy, I wrote a check with a two and four zeros. After acquiring the painting, it hadn't taken long to figure out where the shed had sat in 1869. Getting the officials involved was the toughest sell of all—with good reason, there was no evidence of a crime. Not to mention the many holes in our bizarre, *"Night Circus"* of a tale. A saga with more gut instinct than solid evidence. All we had for proof was my surreal dreams, metamorphosing seagulls, mystical Roses, an enchanting painting, and plenty of apparitions. I'm not even sure, you the reader, believe this tale to be true.

The FBI agents and Fenway where there because of Rachael and as time whisked away, I could see that the stress in her body increased. After forty-five minutes of searching,

Woodard gave Fenway a break as she and Thompson conferred. I detected a problem before the two-person huddle broke and the agents turned towards us. Thompson then approached Rachael and me and said, "The dog is somewhat troubled, but not enough for Woodard to recommend digging up the backyard."

"It's my yard and I'm good with you digging it up."

"It's not that simple, Agent Woodard doesn't want to recommend an official search on such thin evidence, especially without Fenway showing a lot more confidence. She has to think about the reputation of her canine, as well as the cost of deploying the forensic team, the crew, and their equipment. As the property owner, you can hire the equipment and a crew to dig up the backyard; you're free to do as you please. It's your land." said Thompson.

I knew I needed to go easy with Thompson, he was here to help Rachael and I didn't want to create any animosity between us. You never know, we may need his services again. What the job required was the FBI forensic experts. They had the training required to conduct a professional  excavation of a cadaver. I couldn't have a bunch of amateurs sifting through the Cape Cod soil, after all, this was Mary Hartley we were searching for!

"Agent Thompson, I respect your position and that of Woodard's, but I wonder if there can't be a compromise here."

Agent Thompson eyed me with suspicion. After nearly thirty seconds, under his beam like intensity, he said, "Go on."

"My thought is Woodard and Fenway take a break, which isn't unusual. You have one of the forensic experts come through the front door and out to the patio. I'll have the construction crew manually dig up the area where I found the Mason jar while your expert guides them and protects the integrity of the excavation. The heavy equipment won't be used, there'll be no noise to arouse the media. When we find Mary Hartley's skeletal remains, and we will, you can take the credit."

"You're pretty confident there's skeletal evidence where you say it is. But, how are you going to get those guys to dig manually?" asked Thompson.

"The soil is sandy and soft after a foot or so; the digging won't be too strenuous. Plus, I'm going to pay them a lot of money in cash."

"Thompson looked at Rachael with a smile and said, "He's a wily one, this man of yours, are you sure you're ready to marry him?"

Rachael, reciprocated with a wider smile and said, "Wily is exactly what I've been looking for," as she kissed me on my cheek.

A crew of four got to work digging and once they were past the hard, dark topsoil, they cautiously began to remove the orange colored, sandy dirt. The forensic expert, Agent Abigail Blair, guided them with the finesse of a sculptor as they dug deeper into the earth. The process was slow and involved carefully hoeing, shoveling, troweling, and sifting the soil. Three hours later, Agent Blair brushed away loose sandy soil, and exposed the tips of skeletal fingers positioned as if handing someone an object, the size of a Mason jar.

I could hear the voice of Mary saying, "Michael, Michael, thank you. I will love you through eternity, as I know, God will forgive our sin." The sound of these words cast me in the ancient cloth of an Egyptian mummy. I felt entombed, confused. What world had I entered? What sin had I or the other Michael Maine committed! With the excitement of the discovery there was no time for me to concentrate on these thoughts.

Suddenly, everything happened in a flash. Rachael gave me the biggest kiss and best hug anyone could ask for.

Her love freed me from my supernatural thoughts and brought me back to the present.

Agent Thompson had a broad smile on his face, and he showed the full extent exposing his bright, white teeth. The backhoe was started for visual and audio effects. The NASCAR like revving of the big engine brought the media to life. They were impatient, and somewhat rude, demanding a statement from the FBI.

Neither Rachael nor I attended the carnival-like press conference. Agent Thompson was gracious and credited us for tracking down the painting and helping to facilitate the FBI investigation. Woodard and Fenway got the bulk of the credit for identifying the site where Mary's skeleton was located. He also extended gushing kudos to the local police.

The discovery of Mary Hartley after 150 years caused a media frenzy and short-term annoyance for Rachael and me. The television coverage created a hullabaloo at Bunny's and the Mad Dawg Pub for a couple of weeks, then finally died down. Like most front-page stories, ours passed briskly. It wasn't long before we returned to our normal routine, and that was cool with us.

There were now two important events we were preparing for, both joyous in their own way. Once the FBI concluded their investigation, Mary Hartley would finally get her long-held hope for a Christian burial, and Rachael and I would exchange wedding vows.

The evening the excavation concluded; Rachael had sat on the sofa with the little lover boy snuggling next to her. Sailor had abandoned ship again and was like a rubber dinghy trailing in the wake of my girl—my girl, a sound I love to hear. Rachael was spending between three to five nights a week at my place depending on her work schedule. Those nights my little mate was more her dog than mine. When it's just me and the hound, he knows what the skipper expects. He's conditioned to my tempo and quickly becomes shipshape, at least for a day or two.

Rachael was looking up at the empty space over the fireplace mantel. She was literally in shock, but managed to speak and said, "Michael, the painting, it's gone!" In all the excitement of the day, I had forgotten to share my earlier discovery with her. The painting was beautiful, and had finally found a real home, now it was destroyed.

"Rachael, I'm sorry, I noticed it had decayed right before you arrived with the FBI. I woke up on the couch, I was looking at the vacant space but it had only registered subliminally. After my shower I had a sudden realization the painting was gone. Then I ran into the house to make sure I hadn't dreamt it. When I examined the area where we hung the painting all I found was a pile of smut on the mantel."

"Oh, Michael, the beautiful painting; what happened?"

"I don't know, I played the events of the last ten months over in my mind and I'm not sure what to believe. So much of what we've encountered had been shrouded in mystery and mysticism."

"But the legend, the accuracy, without that information; I'm not sure we could have determined the location of the shed."

"I agree, the painting lasted until we were able to find Mary Hartley. Thinking about it now, Rose was right, the search for the painting was a test. Whatever force had challenged us wanted to know if we were committed enough, to honor Mary Hartley's request, before allowing us to obtain the painting. I know it all sounds preposterous, but once the painting served its purpose, wherever it had been buried these past 150 years, the natural elements caused it to decay. I'm not even sure the painting really physically or tangibly existed. Think about it, we've encountered just three people who actually said that they had seen the painting."

"But Michael, it's been hanging in art galleries for many years."

"Rachael, I don't have all the answers, and I don't have any logical explanations for many of the things we've experienced while searching for the painting. Simply finding the Mason jar unbroken after all those years now looks unbelievable. I could make a list of all the strange occurrences we've encountered starting with the mysterious Rose Gallery, Rose Flynn, Roisin, and Rose from The Wishing Well. All four Rose's had spoke of the mysterious person who would one day appear and understand what the painting had to say. And, think about how protective they all were of the painting. You heard Mr. Hartless; Rose refused to show him the painting. Her suspicion about his client, keeping it in her storage room, and denying it existed. Rose wouldn't even accept reasonable offers from people wanting to purchase the painting. My dreams of Mary speaking to me, guiding me, telling me she loved me. My own similar sounding voice telling me to turn the painting around, then finding the hidden legend. I could go on and on listing the strange happenings we had to deal with."

"It's all so unreal."

"I know."

"Rose, Roisin, and Andrew saw the painting. Meg's dove somehow played a part, what is the Avellino connection?"

246

"Rachael I'm not sure, maybe Rose let Andrew see the painting because she trusted him and wanted to believe he could hear what the painting had to say. I don't know how Meg plays into the story, but I'm thankful for her transforming bird. I think we should put it all aside for now, and when the time is right, we can explore this mystery and try to find answers to all of our questions."

"I agree, we should savor our success in locating Mary Hartley. We can dwell on the supernatural events after our honeymoon. Now come over here and cuddle with me."

I tried to nudge the little Spartan off the couch, but the pooch wasn't retreating, so I wedged myself into a small space on the other side. Rachael smiled and said, "I'm surrounded by my two best men." We kissed, not passionately, but romantically. When our lips part, I concentrated on her beautiful face, and told her of my experience the night before we found Mary Hartley's skeletal remains, leaving nothing out.

Rachael's a great listener, and when I finished, she said, "You believed with all your heart you would find Mary Hartley, and you told me you would never forget the victims of the Saxby Gale, and you didn't. I can't explain the events you experienced last night. It could have been a bad dream and you tried to put your rain gear on in your sleep, or there's something to be said of the ghost of Mary Hartley. Now that we found her, she'll have her Christian Service, and will finally rest in peace. We can pull it all together after our wedding and when we return from Provincetown"

We kissed a few more times and when we released, I said, "I'll put my money on the ghost of Mary Hartley, somehow we connected on a spiritual level; her spirit led the way."

Rachael stood up, held my hand and said, "Let's go to bed."

I didn't need much more incentive to push the Hartley mystery out of my mind. I readily complied with Rachael's invitation. Sailor started to follow us, but it only took a firm look from the new boss of the house for the pup to retreat to his bed. It would be awhile before we fell asleep, but we enjoyed every moment of love making until fatigue hit us hard. Rachael was the first to drift off to sleep. My last vision, before I entered into a deep slumber, was the grotesque image of the crazed, Old Man Hartley, holding his shovel.

\*

Over the next couple of weeks, while Rachael worked, I visited funeral homes, Catholic Churches, and cemeteries. The FBI forensic investigators retained the bones and other physical evidence found in my backyard. These scientists attempted to discover cause of death, sex, age of the deceased, as well a host of other forensic evidence. I respect the work of these professionals, and I'm more than grateful for their assistance. For me, there was no doubt, the bones and other fragments that were recovered belonged to Mary Hartley.

When I purchased my home nearly a year ago, I dismissed the legend of the Ghost of Old Man Hartley. Now I am a believer in myths, mysticism, spirits, ghosts, sagas, and folk tales of every kind tied to the supernatural. It seems certain to me, for whatever reason, Mary's ghost connected with me. I became the conduit for her spirit to rise to the surface of the earth and for her skeletal remains to be located.

Rachael and I selected three Catholic Churches for me to recontact for the memorial service for Mary Hartley: Our Lady of the Cape in Brewster, Saint Pius X in South Yarmouth, and Holy Trinity in West Harwich. All three are wonderful venues, and the parish priests were helpful. They all wanted to perform the Catholic service Mary so bravely requested. As Christians, they knew the importance of finding a home for Mary Hartley's soul.

In the end, the selection was relatively easy. Rachael and I wanted to maintain as much historical honesty with the internment of Mary as possible. We had learned from my initial research some interesting facts about the 1860s: first, the Irish represented fifty-six percent of the population in Dennis; second, there was a small community of Irish Catholics in the Mid-Cape area; and third, Catholic Services in Harwich started in 1865.

We knew directly from Mary she was Catholic. While we couldn't state definitively Mary Hartley was of Irish ancestry, based upon the population there was more than a fifty-fifty chance she was. Mrs. Murphy couldn't be one-hundred-percent certain Mary was Irish, but she presumed her to be—both her great-grandmother and Mary attended the same church doing charitable work together.

It appeared to us, from 1865 to 1869, there were two options for attending Catholic services; Sandwich, which began in 1829 and Harwich in 1865. Given the mode of transportation of the time and the conditions of the roads, Harwich was the more likely place for her to have worshiped.

The parish priest for Holy Trinity Church in West Harwich was wonderful. He agreed to conduct the service and add Irish prayers and songs to the ceremony. Once we acquired the skeletal remains of Mary Hartley, we firmed up the date.

My next challenge turned out to be no challenge at all. I was introduced to members of the Harwich Cemetery Commission who were of great assistance. Rachael and I wanted to provide for Mary Hartley as if she were family. With the way our two spirits connected, she certainly felt like an intimate relative. I wanted her soul to have the proper home she'd requested. The perfect place was Mount Pleasant Cemetery in Harwich. The beautiful, old graveyard sits on a knoll overlooking the quaint, nine-hole Harwich Port Golf Course. The cemetery operated for a short time between 1860 to 1869. Rachael and I walked the historic burial ground and it immediately became obvious that Mount Pleasant would be the perfect, final resting place for Mary Hartley. After all, some of the people entombed in the old graveyard must have been her neighbors and friends. The cemetery commissioners were quick to recognize the historical significance; particularly in light of Mary's death during the infamous Saxby Gale of 1869.

The FBI forensic team had the skeletal remains identified as a short, small bone female, roughly 150 years old. There was no discernible trauma or foul play. The cause of death was classified as undetermined. Their findings allowed us to take possession of Mary and bury her in the quaint, serene graveyard next to the old golf course.

When things had finally calmed down, I called Jane from the Historical Society to let her know the Hartley painting had been destroyed. I skipped filling her in on the bizarre details. My next call was to Mrs. Murphy to let her know of the planned memorial service. She was grateful for the call and planned to attend. My final call was to Roisin to let her know about the tragic loss of the Hartley Farm painting. I would like to tell you that I wasn't surprised to learn that the telephone was no longer in service at her fine art gallery, but it wouldn't be the truth. I guess I should have expected it given the odd happenings over the last few months.

Rachael worked the afternoon shift the day before the funeral, so I took a ride to Sandwich. I wanted to again thank Rose for selling me the painting and providing the key to discovering Mary's skeletal remains. I thought she would be interested to know of the religious service scheduled for the morning. I also wanted to check on her health considering how frail she looked as we left her shop. When I arrived at the small gallery, the business appeared abandoned. There was a blank sign above the door, and when I exited my truck and peered through a broken shutter, all the inventory was gone. I checked with the nearby stores and no one could tell me anything of Rose or The Wishing Well. Oddly, as if that word could apply to this tale, no one remembered the business. Others I had spoken with told me they thought it was used for storage. I guess with all the bizarre happenings that occurred during our search, I shouldn't be surprised the store was shuttered or maybe never really existed.

I sat in my truck for some time not quite ready to leave. My gaze was unconscious and kept shifting from the boarded-up store, to the wordless sign above the door. It struck me like a bolt of lightning when I realized the distinct resemblance between Rose of The Wishing Well and Roisin (Little Rose). I hadn't seen Rose from the Rose Gallery, but I guess I didn't really need too. Roisin had said, "Most people thought we were twins."

I don't know how all the pieces of the puzzle specifically fit into this tale, but I'm sure there's an explanation to be discovered. Thinking over our visit to Roisin's shop, I recalled the subtle evasiveness of her comment regarding why she hadn't purchased the Hartley painting. She said without elaboration, "It wasn't meant to be." When I asked her about her likeness to Rose Flynn she'd said, "A distant connection." A distant connection! Suddenly the stunning recollection hit me like a Mohammad Ali punch—the obituary; Rose (Roisin) Flynn! This connection convinced me that the Roses and Roisin are one and the same person.

I couldn't reconcile what Roisin's comments meant to the role she played in the Hartley mystery, but I was convinced she, or the name Roisin, are an important link to solving this saga. While I have no physical evidence, I know how unsettled I felt around Roisin, and her artwork. Thinking about it now, maybe she had the Hartley painting in her shop after all, but I hadn't yet proved I was a worthy enough knight to be given the "Holy Grail."

My best illogical theory was the spirit of Rose Flynn, Mary Hartley's best friend and confidant, was the force behind my finding the painting that had disappeared in 1869. The ghost of the artist, Michael Maine, was the voice that led me to the code written in invisible ink on the back of the Hartley Farm Painting.

These thoughts gave me an odd vibe—reason had given way to emotion, and I felt part of something bigger than myself. Whatever it was, mystical, spiritual, or supernatural, so much had happened during the search for the painting. It was impossible to discern what was real anymore. Another unusual occurrence was the check I wrote to The

Wishing Well when I had purchased the painting hasn't been cashed.

While I was perplexed by the disappearance of the Rose Gallery, Roisin's Fine Art Gallery, and The Wishing Well, I needed to push aside my desire to know more and concentrate on Mary Hartley's Christian funeral. I would save all of the unnatural phenomena for another day.

I'm reluctant to mention this final encounter folks, but full disclosure compels me to tell you. As I was turning the key to start my truck, you probably guessed it, the mysterious seagull who attacked the monster in the reeds landed on the hood of my Ridgeline. The all-white oracle, whose eyes appeared to grow large as he stared at me. His glare sent a shiver through my spine as if someone had scratched a blackboard with long, sharp fingernails.

I quickly relaxed as the bird transformed into a dove. The bird of hope had a short message that penetrated my thoughts, "Tread lightly, Michael Maine...There is more evil in the netherworld than good...Beware the revenge of Old Man Hartley!" Those words sent a rush of fear through my body causing my eyes to blink. When I opened them, the bird was gone and some passerby's had given me an odd look.

I'd once read in mythology that birds are the link between the supernatural and the human world. I appreciated the warning from the cosmic creature, my response to myself—I will return to the phantom world and have my questions answered—I will rely on the mutating bird to guide and protect me on my quest. In the meantime, I positioned Meg Avellino's painting of the transformative seagull prominently over my mantel for a little insurance.

When I later told Rachael about my call to Roisin's gallery and my trip to Sandwich she kept things in perspective and said, "There's no logical explanation for many of the odd occurrences we've encountered while searching for the painting. The Wishing Well mystery and the transforming seagull are two more examples of our bizarre adventure. What's most important, is that we found the painting, located Mary Hartley, and now she'll be laid to rest in the tradition of her faith."

After a good night's sleep, Rachael and I woke up on the morning of the funeral with a renewed hope September change brings. The sun shone bright and the sky was nearly cloudless; it was a perfect day. It was the polar opposite of the night Mary Hartley had died during the peak of the Saxby Gale.

Rachael, Kitten, and I attended the Christian service together. Upon entering the church, we were greeted by an enchanting arrangement of red, white, pink, and yellow roses.

256

The brilliant pigment of the petals made me think of the four Rose's as links in a chain of events that had led us to Mary Hartley. The pastel blooms shone like four apparitions adorned in sweeping, colorful gowns. It was fitting that the manifestation of the four ghostly Roses were in attendance as flowers, since they played an integral part in this mystery. Only later did we learn an anonymous donor, with the now familiar script, MM, had sent the beautiful bouquets of roses or was it Roses.

I stayed transfixed by the beauty of the altar as we joined Mrs. Murphy who sat in the front pew of the church. I didn't mention her great-grandmother's likeness to the Rose who sold me the painting or anything related to our search.

While waiting for the priest to enter the nave and begin his walk toward the altar, I detected a fruity, flowery scent emanating from the burning candles. My mind raced, while I scrutinized the people sitting in the pews hoping to see Rose from The Wishing Well. The church was filled with over two hundred people, but no Rose. The fruity, flowery scent would follow me through the entire religious service.

The priest from Holy Trinity Church did a fine job with the funeral Mass. He delivered a short eulogy praising the courage of Mary Hartley. Once concluded, we discreetly escorted the casket to Mount Pleasant Cemetery where the priest said some final prayers. As Mary's coffin was lowered into her burial plot, dozens of roses that had graced the altar accompanied her into the ground.

Looking around the old, historic cemetery, I heard the voice I recognized as similar to my own say, "Thank you Michael, you did for Mary what I couldn't." I had to smile; I now knew Mary's secret—her love and intimacy with the other Michael Maine!

After over 150 years Mary Hartley's soul had found a home. Her final resting place would be amongst her friends and neighbors. Rachael and I would return many times to lay flowers at the base of her headstone, and the fruity, flowery scent was always present and comforting. I would one day search for the visitants who had guided me to the Hartley painting, but my friends, that is a story for another day.

Rachael and I planned to be married by a Justice of the Peace at ten in the morning, on Monday, the thirtieth of September. My fiancée; folks I can't tell you how many times I had repeated the words, "My fiancée," to myself. An unbelievable sweet sound. My fiancée, I get to say it again, had arranged to be off for a week. We planned a quiet honeymoon trip to Wellfleet, Truro, and Provincetown to explore the Outer Cape.

Rachael didn't want to choose between her coworkers, so Kitten offered to be her maid of honor. All I can say is that she looked stunning in that role. She wore a V-neck, blush toned, floral print, ruffled dress with three-quarter-length sleeves. Watercolor flowers with fading shades of green leaves were splashed over a polyester fabric. The hem fell an inch below the knee exposing her shapely legs. Her hair was short, face had a bronze glow, and she applied only a modest amount of makeup.

Rachael had the beauty of the rising sun. She was adorned in an ivory toned, A-line, scoop neck, knee-length, lace dress. Her dark complexion, wavy hair with a mild windblown look, and large, round, sexy eyes contrasted brilliantly with her outfit.

I know you ladies out there want to know what type of shoes my two best girls were wearing. The truth is, I couldn't take my eyes off the faces of the two most beautiful women to ever venture onto Cape Cod long enough to notice. All I know is, I pulled an Andrew Shepherd line from my favorite movie, *American President,* and complimented my girls on their shoes.

Once the short intimate ceremony was over, we headed to Kitten's house. She had generously offered to host a small party in her home after the wedding service. Rachael had three of her friends from the library in attendance. My guests were Marco, who agreed to be my best man, and Daniel his partner. To be honest, I was kind of embarrassed asking him. We may banter back and forth, and have a good relationship, but we haven't known each other very long. Marco was a good sport and enjoyed his role, telling me, "Anything for a Navy man." Like me, I'm sure you can tell, Marco is truly the best of men.

Kitten's party ended around one in the afternoon. Marco had to return to his service station and Daniel, a physician, had patients scheduled. Rachael's friends had to work the afternoon shift at the library. You know Kitten, she's always hustling to make a buck. Everyone in attendance were wonderful and we greatly enjoyed their company.

Rachael and I headed home, I love the sound of those words, and the thought of building a life together. We were pretty much packed and ready to go, but we couldn't resist taking an outdoor shower together—you know what that lead to. Yikes!

We were on the road before four in the afternoon, heading down 6A. Our adventure began with a lovely ride through Brewster, a scenic and tranquil road we'd taken many times. We entered the rotary in Orleans and picked up the Mid-Cape Highway heading toward Eastham on our way to Provincetown. I'm a pretty safe driver, but I couldn't help stealing gazes at my new bride as we continued on our journey.

We chose to stay at the Lands End Inn because of its scenic view, artistic feel, stained glass windows, and most importantly, it was dog friendly. My mate had the clairvoyance of a psychic. He immediately knew something was going on, so the pooch spent all of his time by Rachael's side as we packed the truck. No way Sailor would miss our departure and allow himself to be left in port. Romantic interlude or not, he made up his mind, he was coming.

I knew three was a crowd on our honeymoon, but hey, I didn't want to be the odd guy out. So, what could I say, you know who was coming. The truth is, we had a great time with the little tyke on our honeymoon, and we were glad he was with us. Sailor is a true beach boy. He loves to sprint to the ocean and dive into the white foam atop the surf. He's a ham to the third degree, he redefines the word frolicking. We loved tiring him out during the day. We didn't need a nosy four-legged voyeur at night, catch my drift!

Rachael had arranged a wonderful trip for us. She loves outdoor activities, nature, and the Cape. Rachael wanted our new family to walk the beaches of the National

Seashore, hike the scenic trails outside of the Nauset Ranger Station, tour the dunes, and visit the lighthouses of Truro and Provincetown.

We're true romantics, we planned to watch the sunsets dipping into the Cape Cod Bay and the sunrises, with the top of its sphere poking up from the waters of the Atlantic Ocean. The Outer Cape has the best of both worlds—sunrises and sunsets; but I love the Town of Dennis.

We had the binoculars packed with our color-coded birder book. You already know Rachael's knowledge of birds and flowers is much superior than mine. She loves the distinct sharp colors of birds and flowers and has embraced my hobby with a passion. She told me she would make me a novice birdwatcher and teach me the names of the colorful wildflowers that I love. I can already feel the heat of her body against mine as she instructs me in the finer points of bird and flower identification. Lesson one, the sole function of a flower is sexual reproduction. See, I'm a fast learner!

Rachael and I are getting close to P-Town, and since more than three really is a crowd, I won't be bringing you along on our honeymoon. In all seriousness, there's one last thought I wanted to share with you. There is hope for this retired sailor, I trust my Rachael, and love her with all my heart and soul.

# 5

It's been a little over a year since I arrived on Cape Cod. I'm
standing on the jetty at West Dennis Beach, the day is sunny

and bright. There's a soft breeze drifting in from Nantucket Sound. The weather today is as perfect as my life.

When I look back to last year and that rainy September night, standing strong, holding the night watch at the end of the wet, slick, rocky, jetty; letting the rain beat on me like the hailstones from a winter gale; I knew the road I would take and the new home I had found was the right choice. For me, there was no other road that "equally lay."

There was never any buyer's remorse for this sailor and no other path for "another day." I will never "sigh." For the first time in my life, I know my roots are firmly planted in solid soil; in a place where I know I belong.

Rachael is my heart and soul. She is my soulmate, muse, and my strength. We will build a family together, and as we grow older our love will remain young. Her smile, her lips, and the love we make will sustain me forever. She completes my life; my wandering is over.

I love my life, and I don't know if the road I took was "less traveled," but the road I took "made all the difference."

Made in the USA
Middletown, DE
22 August 2020

16055854R00158